This book is a powerful and spellbinding story of how the Lord directs and is concerned about every detail of our lives. The Lord gifted Cecilia with the ability to communicate a story from His Word that directly relates to our own. I was moved to tears to watch the unfolding of God's mercy upon a life that was devastated and seemingly destroyed. I was uplifted, encouraged and fascinated at how the Lord turned a great tragedy into a great blessing. I felt The Lord stir in my own heart promise and assurance He IS DOING the same for me...and He is doing the same for you. This is a great book for everyone, but especially those who need affirmation of God's Providence and Redemption.

— Debbie Stuart, author *20 Minutes A Day*, Former Director of Women's Ministry at Prestonwood Baptist Church, Ministry Leader for Women of Faith and currently serving as Director of Ministry Initiatives at Hope for the Heart

Going Home is a retelling of one of my favorite stories, Naomi and Ruth. It is lovingly retold by Cecilia Bacon, and I hope she will retell more biblical stories. It is a story of love, friendship, hope and redemption. A lovely, gentle read!

— Leanna Ellis, award winning author of *Facelift*

Going HOME

A STORY OF RUTH AND NAOMI

CECILIA BACON

WESTBOW
PRESS®
A DIVISION OF THOMAS NELSON
& ZONDERVAN

Scripture taken from the Holy Bible, NEW INTERNATIONAL VERSION®.
Copyright © 1973, 1978, 1984 by Biblica, Inc. All rights reserved worldwide.
Used by permission. NEW INTERNATIONAL VERSION® and NIV® are
registered trademarks of Biblica, Inc. Use of either trademark for the offering
of goods or services requires the prior written consent of Biblica US, Inc.

WestBow Press books may be ordered through booksellers or by contacting:

WestBow Press
A Division of Thomas Nelson & Zondervan
1663 Liberty Drive
Bloomington, IN 47403
www.westbowpress.com
1 (866) 928-1240

Because of the dynamic nature of the Internet, any web addresses or
links contained in this book may have changed since publication and
may no longer be valid. The views expressed in this work are solely those
of the author and do not necessarily reflect the views of the publisher,
and the publisher hereby disclaims any responsibility for them.

Any people depicted in stock imagery provided by Thinkstock are
models, and such images are being used for illustrative purposes only.
Certain stock imagery © Thinkstock.

ISBN: 978-1-4908-8482-0 (sc)
ISBN: 978-1-4908-8483-7 (hc)
ISBN: 978-1-4908-8481-3 (e)

Library of Congress Control Number: 2015909696

Print information available on the last page.

WestBow Press rev. date: 7/27/2015

Contents

This book is dedicated to all the ladies out there who are seeking restoration for their brokenness.

> For everyone who asks receives; the one who seeks finds; and to the one who knocks, the door will be opened.

(Luke 11:10)

Preface

This book started when I was preparing to facilitate a study on Ruth in a women's Bible study group at my church. As a study leader, I find it's important to read the study before I teach it and to stay a few lessons ahead of those taking the class. This time, before I jumped into the material, I decided to read the book of Ruth in the Bible.

It was certainly not the first time I had read this book, but it suddenly felt like it was! What surprised me was that I began to see my own personal life threaded throughout the story line. When I looked closely at each of the characters, I saw my own weaknesses and vulnerabilities, but I also saw how God redeemed these characteristics and turned them around to his glory.

In order to engage the ladies, each week I began writing little stories about the characters to bring a more personal perspective into the study. What they didn't know was that each story was a snapshot of myself. The stories I wrote were so well received that I felt encouraged to expand them and string them together when the study ended.

My hope is that this love story will encourage all who read it to open their Bibles and look for themselves in the words. I believe when you do that, you will find yourself, and you will also find a personal message or lesson that God has just for you. After all, the Bible is the greatest love story of them all!

Acknowledgments

There are so many I'd like to thank for encouraging me to get to this point, starting with my Lord and Savior, Jesus Christ. Without him, my eyes would have remained closed and my life would have stayed broken. My world has never been the same since I said yes to him, even though admittedly there are days when I prefer to keep my eyes tightly closed!

Secondly, I want to thank the love of my life, my husband Danny. He is the one who believes in me even when I don't believe in myself. He not only loves me unconditionally, but he taught me how to laugh—which also includes the ability to laugh at myself. Believe me, I can be a little intense sometimes, so learning to laugh was critical!

Of the utmost importance are the ladies in my life. Whether it is a forever "sister" or a "sister" for a season, I can't thank you enough. It's *you* who drives me by either challenging me to step forward in my journey or by challenging me to tell you how much I love my Jesus and how much I want you to love him too.

A special thank-you goes out to two ladies who have prayed me through this book: Cora and Trudy. Without your encouragement and prayers, I would never have had the courage to take this step.

Finally, to my sister Terry, thank you for never giving up on me and praying for me to come to know the Lord in spite of my anger and rebellion. When I was so overwhelmed about how I was ever going to know who this Jesus was, thank you for gently guiding me through the Word in multiple translations. You know the darkest secrets about me, yet you still love and encourage me. Who but you would listen to my whining and confidences for hours every week? (PS. We still have that pact of silence, right?)

Eternally grateful to you all,
Cecilia

Now Elimelech, Naomi's husband, died, and she was left with her two sons. They married Moabite women, one named Orpah and the other Ruth. After they had lived there about ten years, both Mahlon and Kilion also died, and Naomi was left without her two sons and her husband.

(Ruth 1:3–5)

Chapter 1

NAOMI

It was late afternoon when all those who had come to mourn with them finally departed. Naomi sat in her bedroom chair, looking out the window but not really seeing. In all her life, she had never felt so numb, so devoid of emotion. First, her husband's death, and now, both of her sons were gone. In the blink of an eye, she and the girls were all alone and destitute.

The house was silent except for her sons' wives, Ruth and Orpah, who were busy cleaning and sweeping in the outer room. Naomi could hear one of the girls crying quietly, and without turning around to look, she was certain it was Orpah. The girl had not stopped crying since they had received the news about the accident. Ruth, although distraught in the beginning, had gotten her emotions under control and had taken charge of everything. She graciously received all the townswomen as they had trickled in and out over the past few weeks.

Naomi could barely function. The shock and grief of the terrible loss made her body feel like she was walking through a thick fog, scarcely able to move without assistance from one of the girls. She had not uttered a word since that terrible morning when the foreman delivered the news of her sons' death.

Still not moving, the older woman lifted her eyes and gazed at the blue sky with the fluffy clouds lazily floating by her window; she felt the warmth of the sun settle on her body. She thought, *How can this day be so normal when nothing is normal?*

Her mind traveled back over the morning and how at one point she had had to restrain herself from jumping up from her chair and ordering everyone to leave her home. Words! Meaningless words spoken to her by so many women who really had no way of understanding how she felt. She wanted them to leave her home and not talk to her because they didn't understand! They couldn't possibly understand.

Naomi's anger quickly turned back to heartbreak, and she tried to hold back a sob, but grief escaped her—a woeful sound in the silence.

There was only one thing that broke through her numbness today, and it was overhearing a woman whisper to Ruth that perhaps Naomi should return to her own country. The woman had heard there was no longer a famine in Bethlehem. Naomi couldn't stop thinking about those words. Could it be? Had God remembered her people?

She shook herself slightly and her anger flared again. In her heart, she screamed, *Well, God has forgotten me! He left me a widow and childless. I have nothing! We have nothing!* Hot tears began streaming down her face and dripped onto hands that had become clenched into fists in her lap.

Naomi knew that staying in Moab would be dangerous and could even mean death for her and her daughters-in-law. As widows left alone with not one man to care for them, they would most certainly be beggars soon and die in the streets. Worse would befall the girls if their families refused to take them back into their homes.

A slight breeze broke through the window, cooling the tears that descended her face. The breeze was so soft and gentle it began to feel like a touch, like someone gently caressing Naomi's face and arms. She felt a shiver run down her spine as she rapidly blinked her eyes, remembering precious touches from her husband and sons.

In spite of her clouded thoughts, she heard what sounded like faint whispers. At first, she decided she would ignore them, but the whispers seemed so persistent somehow. Slightly annoyed, Naomi leaned forward in her chair and peeked over the window ledge to see if someone was outside, but she saw no one. Yet she could still hear the whispers.

Curious now, she placed her hands on the edge of the window and strained her body and ears while trying to catch the words floating in and out of the breeze. Her entire soul felt a sudden restlessness with a deep longing. Closing her eyes and focusing intentionally on the whispers, all at once she clearly heard one word repeated over and over, and it seemed to swirl and wrap around her body: *home.*

The word was spoken in a voice that gave her comfort rather than fear. And it was so barely audible that, had it not been quiet in the house, she would have missed it.

There was no mistaking what Naomi heard, and her heart quickened its beat. She continued to lean forward in an attempt to catch more, but it seemed all she heard was the same word circling around her, enveloping her body and mind with a clear direction.

Home. Naomi took in a deep, cleansing breath, slowly exhaled, and knew deep in her heart what she must do.

Chapter 2

RUTH

Ruth and Orpah were setting the house in order and putting things away after all the townswomen had finally left for the day. Ruth worked in silence, but Orpah cried softly. Naomi was sitting silently at the window, and Ruth thought her heart would break seeing her mother's pain. Although now a widow herself, she knew that her pain was nothing compared to the loss a mother endures.

In the silence, a sob escaped Naomi, and the girls stopped what they were doing to look at their mother-in-law, the woman Ruth had come to think of as Mother. Would she invite an embrace from them? Both girls knew that unless she did, it was best they keep their distance. Ruth could feel herself holding her breath as she waited for Naomi to turn and open her arms to them, but after a few moments, Ruth sighed and went back to work.

As Ruth swept the hard floor, she felt a twinge of guilt because she wasn't experiencing the same sense of despair as Naomi and Orpah. Of course, the news of her husband's death was devastating, but after the initial shock, she had a sense of peace covering her that she really didn't know how to put into words. Somehow, Ruth knew everything was going to be okay, and she longed to share this feeling with Naomi.

The young Moabitess had never had a close relationship with her own mother, so Naomi's attention and wisdom during her marriage to Mahlon had become precious to the girl. Ruth especially liked to hear stories about Naomi's life back in their home in Israel and about her God. Ruth's family had many gods, but Naomi worshipped only what she called "the one true God." Ruth never tired of hearing the stories about this God even though she didn't understand how Naomi could worship a God she couldn't see.

Ruth knew in the depths of her soul that something was about to change, and it was more than the obvious that they were all widows who were destitute with a very bleak future. No, this change was going to be for the better, and she had nothing more than a heartfelt peace to support her belief. She was both confused and excited, and she longed to sit with Naomi to share her feelings and ask her mother what she thought. How could she have such a feeling of calm when their circumstances meant nothing but a dire future for the women?

Still, how could she speak of these thoughts at such a time as this? Naomi would consider her a callous daughter-in-law, and she herself felt very insensitive thinking such things. Although Naomi and the girls had enjoyed many times of talking and sharing when their husbands were alive, Ruth knew that Naomi needed time to grieve and be comforted. Her thoughts would have to wait.

When Orpah left the room, Ruth stopped sweeping and looked lovingly at her mother. A slight breeze drifted through the windows and brought coolness to Ruth's body in the afternoon heat. She closed her eyes, leaning slightly on the broom and welcoming the coolness that passed over her.

Ruth wasn't sure how long she had been standing there when she heard a breathless whisper. Thinking it to be Naomi beckoning her, her body snapped to attention, her eyes opened, and she started to move, but her feet didn't want to cooperate. She looked toward Naomi, who was still seated but leaning toward the window with her hands on the ledge as if looking at something, but her eyes were closed. She seemed to be drinking in the sunshine.

Ruth decided she must have heard townspeople outside the window, although she thought it strange that she would hear whispers inside their home. She shook herself and started to get back to work, but she heard it again, and this time, it was very clear in the air that swirled around her. One word that was scarcely audible, but Ruth heard it, and chills traveled down her body in spite of the afternoon heat: *home*.

Her heart began beating wildly. Looking at Naomi, she thought, *What can it mean?* She was terrified!

Chapter 3

STEP OF FAITH

Naomi stood up from the chair, and the room seemed to spin around her for a moment. The weeks of inactivity and barely eating had left her body weak, but Naomi never felt more determined.

"Ruth! Orpah!" she called loudly as she held on to her chair for support. Both girls rushed to her side and grabbed her arms in the fear she would fall. Naomi assured them she was going to be fine and instructed them to lead her to the kitchen.

"Girls, you will prepare a meal, and we will talk about our future."

Orpah hung her head and tears began to fall again. Ruth released Naomi's arm and ran back to the bedroom and brought Naomi her chair saying, "Orpah and I will prepare whatever you want Mother, but you sit." Naomi, feeling energized, wanted to stand, but her legs were trembling so she decided to do as Ruth suggested.

The two young women worked together quickly to prepare the meal, but both of them kept a constant watch on their mother. They were surprised at the way Naomi directed them in food preparation with such clarity after weeks of silence. Orpah became so busy she stopped crying.

Ruth prepared the bowls with their thick soup and filled the pitcher with wine, taking them to their mats. Orpah tore big chunks of the bread into a basket and then taking Naomi's hand, led her to the mat so they could eat together.

Once they were seated, Naomi reached out to take the girls' hands. She said, "We will pray."

Both girls bowed their heads and closed their eyes. Neither fully understood Naomi's religion or her God, but they knew from years of being married to her sons, reverence to this God was expected.

Naomi spoke in strength, "God in heaven, the one who created us and who loves us in spite of our iniquities. God, you are the Father of Abraham and all my people, I have heard your call today, and I will obey. I pray that you guide me in the steps we need to take to follow your command."

Ruth's eyes flew open wide, and she raised her head to look at her mother. As Naomi continued to pray for wisdom, Ruth knew in that moment that Naomi had surely heard the same whisper that she herself had heard.

Then Ruth turned her head to look at Orpah for her reaction. Orpah's head was bowed, yet her eyes were open, and she was picking at a spot on her tunic, clearly not listening to Naomi's prayer. Based on her indifference, Ruth felt she had probably not heard the whispers. She wondered whether it was because Orpah hadn't been nearby.

Naomi spoke "Amen" and raised her head to look at her daughters. "We will eat!" she commanded. Naomi's appetite was strong, and this prompted Ruth and Orpah to eat a hearty meal as well. Once the meal was finished, the mats cleared, and the dishes washed, the girls sat back down with Naomi on the mat.

Naomi finally spoke. "Tonight we will sleep and get rest, for tomorrow we will make preparations to return to my homeland."

Orpah's eyes opened wide in surprise, and she began to cry again while Ruth smiled and nodded her head in obedience. They were going home.

Chapter 4

ACTING IN FAITH

> When she heard in Moab that the Lord had come to the aid of his people by providing food for them, Naomi and her daughters-in-law prepared to return home from there. With her two daughters-in-law she left the place where she had been living and set out on the road that would take them back to the land of Judah.
>
> (Ruth 1:6–7)

Once Naomi told the girls they were moving back to her home in the land of Judah, the days had flown by for all of them.

Ruth was shocked at the life that seemed to have been breathed back into her mother. Naomi was focused and steadfast as she guided the girls to prepare for the long journey. She kept the girls busy from sunup until long after the sun went down as they cooked and packed what Naomi determined would be going with them. They also determined what they would leave behind as gifts for friends and what needed to be sold to help with money needed for the journey.

In the ten years that Naomi had lived in Moab, she had not made many friends, but she was well known as a fair and honest woman, and she had the respect of many. Several in town had stopped by and offered gifts to Naomi for the journey when they heard the women were leaving. Each time a gift was received, it was something that Naomi needed—confirmation for her that God was behind her decision to return home.

Yesterday a local merchant, Ish-tob, had stopped by when he heard they were making the long journey back to Judah. He told Naomi that he and his caravan would be traveling much of the same distance as the women intended to take, so they could travel with him. As safety was a major concern for Naomi, his offer was quickly accepted. Unlike many in Moab, Ish-tob was a good man and she knew they would be safe.

Naomi was a woman of small stature and stocky, although her countenance made many think of her as a much more impressive woman. Her square face seemed a bit gaunt from the weight she had lost as she grieved the loss of her sons. Although frail at the start of the week, the hard work and food had quickly helped her regain much of her physical strength. Her eyes were dark and sharp with intelligence, and no one was surprised at her decision to return home as she was known around the city as a practical woman.

Naomi was aloof with the people of Moab, but she easily communicated the state of her heart by the fire of intensity in her eyes when angered or driven, and by the softness of compassion when she looked at those who gained her favor. If a man or woman had a true need, it was known throughout the city that Naomi was a woman who would help if it were possible.

Her hair was thick and wavy, still dark but heavily peppered with strands of white throughout. Her practicality even extended to the keeping of her hair, which she kept brushed back, braided, and wound into a knot at the nape of her neck.

She stood with her hands on her hips in the main room, overlooking the rugs that held the various items they hoped to sell. Her face was lined with deep wrinkles from the sun and the years of hard work she had taken on once her husband had died. Naomi rarely smiled anymore. When she did, it looked more like a grimace, as if she had forgotten how to be happy. Such was the look that was now on her face; she was tired but satisfied with all they had accomplished.

Naomi had sent Orpah and Ruth into town to let the other women know that they were selling many household items. In addition, they were asking the women to let their husbands know about the livestock she needed to sell. Naomi knew she and the girls would need the money to purchase the provisions, food, and wine they would require for the journey home.

Before long, those same townswomen who had come to pay their respects, returned to look over and purchase what she had set out. By the end of the next day, all the items and livestock had been sold. There was enough money to purchase everything they would need for the long journey, with a small amount left over to purchase a few provisions when they arrived in Bethlehem.

***

That night Naomi sat with the girls over the final meal they would have in their home in Moab. She was happy that Orpah had stopped crying all the time, but she could see the girl had become a little more sad and distant as the day was ending.

"Orpah, have you packed everything? Have you checked the roof to make sure we have gotten all of our supplies?" Naomi asked her.

"Yes, Mother," was all the girl would reply.

"Ruth, have you checked all the packing to make sure it is secure and ready to load on the carts?"

Ruth said, "Yes, Mother. I've loaded many of the larger items on the cart, and we have but a few things left to add. Once we finish loading our final things, I have the blankets and ropes prepared to tie everything securely onto the cart in the morning." She smiled at Naomi, unable to contain her excitement for the journey.

Naomi loved both Orpah and Ruth, yet she couldn't deny in her heart that Ruth was more special to her. Both girls were lovely, but Orpah more so, with her curly black hair, a beautiful heart-shaped face with full lips, and a very curvaceous figure. Even while married to Kilion, Orpah still gained the attention of many men in the town.

Lately Naomi noticed men hanging around their home. Most did not have good intentions as they were men who bought women for temple prostitutes. Naomi's silent and cold stare was enough to make them all continue on their way.

Orpah's mother had stopped by early that day and hugged her daughter long and hard. "Daughter," she said to Orpah with tears, "I wish you well. Please take this idol of Chemosh and pray daily for a husband and children. Make sacrifices to our god as often as possible so that you may be married again soon and have many children." Both women embraced and wept together.

"I will, Mother," Orpah said through her tears, clinging strongly to her mother.

Naomi, watching the entire exchange, sharply said, "You will do no such thing! Give that idol back to your mother. We will worship the God of Israel, and not a wooden idol."

Naomi looked at Orpah and her mother with such sternness that both Moabite women knew this topic was not open for discussion. This angered Orpah's mother, and she took the idol back into her hands. Although she didn't argue with Naomi, her eyes showed how much she loathed the Israeli woman.

Never taking her eyes off of Naomi, she said to Orpah, "Daughter, on your behalf, I will daily sacrifice and pray for another husband and many children." She gave Naomi a dark look, hugged her daughter long and hard, and turned to leave. Orpah watched her until she could no longer see her, sobbing all the while.

Ruth, silently watching the exchange, went to Orpah and put her arms around her shoulders, and spoke softly and lovingly to the girl as she brought her back into their home and tried to assure her that everything was going to be all right.

Ruth was a tall and slender woman with large dark eyes and very thick, dark hair that she wore in a braid that ran down to her waist. While she was not beautiful like Orpah, she was quite handsome. Her beauty was such that it seemed to grow the longer you came to know her as she was such a gentle, loving, and kind woman.

Naomi knew there would be no family visits for Ruth, and she was thankful. Ruth's father and brother were known throughout the town for being evil and corrupt. Long after the young girl had joined their household, Naomi suspected that Ruth had been the victim more than once of a beating from a father and brother who drank and gambled too much. Ruth's mother was cowered and timid, and she bore the marks of regular beatings. Naomi knew the woman would not come to see Ruth and risk displeasure from her husband and son.

Naomi allowed Ruth to be tender with Orpah for a few more minutes, then clapping her hands, put both girls back to work with the final packing.

***

The time for departure had finally arrived. Naomi's oxen cart was packed to overflowing and two donkeys were tied behind the cart as they followed Ish-tob's caravan. Naomi had sold most of their livestock save for a few sheep, and Ruth kept them banded together behind the cart with her staff. Naomi walked in front of the cart with Orpah, leading the ox behind her.

As the women passed through the city gates of Moab, Naomi looked back over her shoulder and she was at once excited and nervous. She was going home! Naomi actually smiled for the first time in a long time, and she walked with a sense of purpose toward her home.

It was a beautiful day, and the sun had just started coming up on the horizon. There was a slight breeze, and the two young women chatted softly back and forth to each other as they steadily moved on the road directly behind Ish-tob's large caravan.

They had traveled about an hour, and Naomi seemed to have lost her enthusiasm for the journey and had become very quiet. She kept turning to look at Ruth and Orpah, almost as if to check to see if they were still behind her.

Ruth began to feel a nervous tension build inside herself, and her stomach began to churn. Something was wrong with Naomi. Determined to bring good spirits back to her mother, she called out, "Mother, can you tell us how long we will journey?" Naomi turned and held up her hand for them to stop.

Orpah pushed back on the ox yoke to stop the beast's plodding movement, and Ruth stopped as well. The sheep obediently slowed and gathered nearby, happy for the opportunity to graze. Ruth looked at Naomi and said, "Why are we stopping, Mother?"

Naomi placed her hand on the side of her own face, and she looked first at Ruth and then Orpah, as if she was truly seeing them both for the first time. Almost inaudibly, Naomi responded, "I believe we will be there in about three to four days."

The girls looked at each other, then back at Naomi. It was obvious something was terribly wrong with her. Ruth wondered, *Has she changed her mind? Are we about to turn back and return to Moab?* The sick feeling in the pit of her stomach grew, and for the first time tears began to build in her eyes.

As Naomi continued to look at Orpah and Ruth, she knew she was making a terrible mistake bringing them with her. Boldly she said, "Go back, each of you, to your mother's home" (Ruth 1:8) Ruth and Orpah gasped, and both girls began to cry.

Naomi walked up to the girls as she reached out to touch both of them. She loved her daughters, but taking them back to Bethlehem was a terrible mistake. With love and a deep compassion in her voice, she began to cry and choked out, "May the Lord show kindness to each of you, as you have shown to your dead and to me. May the Lord grant that each of you will find rest in the home of another husband" (Ruth 1:8–9). Then she quickly kissed and embraced them as tears streamed down her face.

Ruth and Orpah wept loudly and said to her, "No, Mother, we will go back with you to your people!"

But Naomi shook her head and touched their shoulders saying, "Return home, my daughters. Why would you come with me? Am I going to have any more sons, who could become your husbands? And even if I received a husband tonight and had sons, would you wait for them to grow up to remarry or remain unmarried for them? No, my daughters. It is more bitter for me than for you, because the Lord's hand has gone out against me. You must go home."

Both daughters wept openly and professed their desire to stay with Naomi. Naomi knew that if their mothers did not take them back, their lives were bleak at best. But she also knew that she could not bring Moabite women back to Judah with her! Not only were they a testimony to her family's disobedience to God and her own shame, but their lives could actually be in danger in her homeland. God was very clear that her people were not to associate with or marry Moabites, and in her haste to return home she had almost forgotten about this. No! She could not take them with her.

Naomi loved Ruth and Orpah, but she tenderly encouraged them with more hugs and kisses to turn around and return to their families. Orpah, weeping loudly, kissed Naomi and turned back home to Moab, but Ruth clung to her.

With a stern tone in her voice Naomi pushed Ruth back away from her and said, "Look, your sister-in-law is going back to her people and her gods. Go back with her."

But Ruth replied, "Don't urge me to leave you or to turn back from you. Where you go I will go, and where you stay I will stay. Your people will be my people and your God my God. Where you die I will die, and there I will be buried. May the Lord deal with me, be it ever so severely, if anything but death separates you and me" (Ruth 1:16–17).

Naomi realized in that moment as she looked deeply into the young woman's eyes that Ruth was determined to go with her. She truly loved Ruth and having the girl with her would be a blessing in many ways, but she could also face severe consequences for bringing a Moabitess with her into Bethlehem.

Yet Naomi also knew Ruth's family. Many times Naomi had marveled at how such a sweet and tender young woman could have come from such a wicked home. Naomi knew it was unlikely that Ruth's family would take her back in, and unless she found a husband today, she would become a beggar or her own father would sell her as a temple prostitute.

"It will not be easy for you in Bethlehem, Ruth." Naomi narrowed her eyes at the young woman, but Ruth remained where she was, her face set in determination.

Ruth looked deeply into Naomi's eyes and with unwavering courage and love she said, "I am going with you, Mother. I know it will be hard for me in your homeland, but it will be worse for me if I return to Moab and my family. You are my only family, yet I vow to you today that I would rather be called and treated as your servant girl rather than return to what awaits me in Moab."

Naomi's stomach felt sick, and she finally nodded her head as she knew Ruth spoke the truth. She reached forward and squeezed Ruth's shoulder and said, "Let us get moving so we may catch up with Ish-tob. It is not good for us to be separated." Naomi grabbed the ox cart yoke and pulled and clicked her tongue at the animal to begin moving while Ruth gathered the sheep with her staff to get the grazing animals moving as well. Before long, they were back near Ish-tob's caravan.

***

The journey to Bethlehem was not easy. The mountainous terrain and the crossing of the river Jordan made it difficult for the two women and for the livestock. Ruth, however, loved the journey and felt she had never seen such blue skies; she was in awe of the majestic mountains and the beautiful trees. She talked nonstop to Naomi about how lovely everything was and of her excitement for their new beginning.

The men in the caravan helped a great deal when the travel became difficult, but Naomi noticed they watched Ruth with intense and open interest and longing. At night when they stopped, the men would sit around the fire and watch the women, and some would beckon Ruth to come and sit with them. Their comments would cause Ruth's face to flush a deep red, and she ducked her face and turned from them, wrapping her shawl around her head and much of her face. Ish-tob would eventually silence them, but Naomi noticed that he spent just as much time watching Ruth, and his interest in her was openly evident.

Because of this, Naomi never left Ruth's side as they ate or tended their livestock, and she lay with her bedroll right next to Ruth's each evening, saying silent prayers to God to protect them.

As they neared Bethlehem, Ish-tob stopped his caravan while his men watered the livestock and waited on him to return so they could continue their journey. The merchant gave Naomi and Ruth final directions for their journey as he was heading on to Joppa.

Both women bowed their heads to him in respect, and Naomi said, "I cannot thank you enough, my lord, for seeing us safely this far. I have only a few coins left from the sale of my household items and livestock before leaving Moab, but I will gladly give you all to repay your kindness."

Ish-tob was silent as he looked at Naomi, seeming to consider her offer. He turned his head to look at Ruth intensely, causing the girl to blush and lower her eyes as she lifted her shawl to cover her head and face. He looked back at Naomi, and nodded his head toward the young woman. He said, "She will not be welcome in your homeland."

Naomi knew the words he spoke had a ring of truth, but she said nothing. Instead, she stood silently before the man, hoping her unwillingness to answer him would make him leave the women to continue their journey.

"I will purchase her from you."

She was stunned at his offer to purchase Ruth that was stated in front of the girl as if she had no more comprehension or value than livestock! Ruth gasped in fear and her heart began beating wildly; she began to tremble violently. Ruth knew if the man decided he would take her, there was nothing she or Naomi could do to stop him.

Naomi stepped closer to Ish-tob and drew her shoulders up, never taking her eyes from his as she carefully considered her response in spite of her secret desire to verbally lash out at him. She knew he could maim or kill her, take Ruth and all of their belongings, and none of his men would stop him. She also knew she needed to be mindful not to bring shame to him with her response.

Lowering her voice so his men would not hear the exchange she said, "My lord, while I thank you for your kind offer, as you can see, I am not a young woman and you know that we are widows and I am too old for marriage." Naomi paused keeping her eyes directly locked on Ish-tob's. "While what you say is true, I will need Ruth to help me when I return home. Our people will allow her to serve me and glean from the fields to provide for us.

"As a man of business, I know you understand my need to have her help at my age. In exchange for your help, which was generous and plentiful on our journey, I will give you the money and all that we have instead." Naomi held her breath and prayed silently to God that he would take her offer.

Without looking up, Ruth knew the merchant was still looking at her, but she kept her eyes lowered, her cheeks aflame, barely breathing. Naomi could see the lust in his face was strong as she watched his internal struggle with Naomi's refusal to sell the girl and his desire to have her.

Finally he looked away from Ruth and to Naomi he said, "I will take nothing. My offer was nothing more than to make your acceptance back into Bethlehem easier." Naomi bowed her head before the man, but she knew that God had intervened on Ruth's behalf, and she slowly exhaled.

As the merchant bid them farewell, Naomi and Ruth respectfully bowed before Ish-tob. Naomi, with sincere gratitude, said, "I pray that God will richly bless you for your kindness, for allowing us to journey with you these past days and for keeping us safe." He dismissed her comments with a wave of his hand and called to his caravan to begin moving again toward Joppa.

Naomi stood in silence for quite some time, watching the caravan until she was certain they would not return. Ruth stood silently behind her and watched as well, afraid that any movement from her would cause the man to have a change of heart and snatch her away from Naomi. When it was evident the men would not return to harm them, Naomi turned to Ruth and said, "Let us continue before it gets dark."

Chapter 5

PRIDE & BITTERNESS

> So the two women went on until they came to
> Bethlehem. When they arrived in Bethlehem, the
> whole town was stirred because of them, and the
> women exclaimed, "Can this be Naomi?"
>
> (Ruth 1:19)

Naomi's fear and concerns began to heighten with each step closer
to Bethlehem. She remembered when she and Elimelech had left
with their sons, they had received a tearful and loving send-off.
They had so much wealth, and now she was returning to her
homeland with almost nothing. In fact, both women's tunics were
dirty and a bit tattered from the journey, and they looked like
beggars in Naomi's eyes.

Pride and bitterness began to grow in her heart, and she began a
stream of negative self-talk to prepare herself and defend her losses
to anyone she might encounter at the city gates. Her biggest concern
was that the elders at the entrance to the gate would not even let
them into town because she was bringing a foreigner with her. She
silently pleaded to God that no one she knew would see her or Ruth
arrive, and they would be able to get to her old home unnoticed.

It was a beautiful morning, and the city was busy with commerce entering into and out of the gates of Bethlehem. It seemed to Ruth that there was a glow about the city, and everything looked clean—even the smells coming from the city inside the gates were not offensive like in Moab.

Naomi looked at Ruth and gruffly said, "Stay close to me. Cover your face as much as possible; do not bring attention to yourself and do not speak."

Ruth looked at her mother, and she knew that Naomi was ashamed of her, and for that her heart pinched with pain. She wrapped her shawl over her head and around the lower part of face, obscuring all but her eyes from view, but it didn't stop Naomi from seeing the hurt she had inflicted on the girl. For a moment Naomi felt sorry for her words and almost took them back, but she hardened her heart and told herself what she asked was for Ruth's protection.

Naomi picked up the pace, and they briskly walked through the gates and into the city. Ruth kept her eyes on Naomi while trying to keep their sheep close by the cart. It seemed like Naomi was trying to rush through the city, and Ruth felt that her haste was bringing more attention to them than if had she made a leisurely entrance. But she didn't say a word to Naomi about her thoughts.

Nearby were a group of townswomen, chatting and laughing after a morning of shopping. Their children played around them nearby, running in and out of the busy shopping areas. The sound of Naomi's hurried cart caught one woman's attention, and she glanced over at them before returning to the conversation. Then all at once, her eyes opened wide and she spoke loudly, "Can this be Naomi?"

The women stopped talking and turned to look at Naomi. Once Naomi realized the townswomen had spied her, she slowed down her pace. Some of the women she did not know, but many were old and dear friends. One woman named Varda started toward her with arms open and joy in her voice saying, "Naomi? Is it you, my friend?"

Naomi had no choice but to stop and greet the women. With a tearful and harsh voice, she said to them, "Don't call me Naomi. Call me Mara, because the Almighty has made my life very bitter. I went away full, but the Lord has brought me back empty. Why call me Naomi? The Lord has afflicted me; the Almighty has brought misfortune upon me" (Ruth 1:20–21).

The women were silent, and her friend stopped in her tracks, not daring to come near Naomi or Ruth. Varda knew in an instant that Naomi coming home alone and with a young girl meant something unthinkable had happened to the men in her family, and her heart broke. For now, she would give Naomi the space she obviously wanted and needed.

Naomi looked at the women one final time, her face hard, and with harsh words turned to Ruth and said, "Girl, let us continue."

Ruth looked at the townswomen, and she saw nothing but kindness in the eyes of the women, and especially in the woman who had spoken to her mother. She wanted to encourage Naomi to reach out to them and to accept an embrace from them. Instead, she obeyed Naomi's initial command not to speak and continued to herd the sheep, following behind Naomi.

At one point, Ruth looked over her shoulder back to the women, and they all continued to stand together and watch her and Naomi. The older woman who tried to embrace Naomi raised a hand in farewell, but Ruth was fearful of what Naomi would say, so she dropped her head and turned her attention back to the animals.

***

Naomi and Ruth got to work unloading the cart, and they placed their belongings inside Naomi's old home. Many people stopped to look and stare, but the cold looks from Naomi caused the curious to move along. After all their things had been moved inside, the older woman stood at the doorway, her hands pressed together covering her mouth, her eyes darted around in the dim light of the room. She surveyed her abandoned home, so familiar and yet so strange. Before old memories began to threaten tears, she turned to Ruth and instructed her to go into town to sell the ox and cart.

"There is a merchant in town who buys and sells livestock. His name is Ike, and he will buy our cart and ox. Because you are a stranger, he will try to give you a low price, but tell him they belong to Naomi who has returned to her home. He will give you a fair price. After he pays you, purchase a bag of meal from him for our animals. You must go quickly and return before it gets dark." She gave Ruth directions to reach his booth in the city.

Ruth was petrified, but did as her mother asked. Leading the beast and cart slowly through the noisy market, she watched as the people transacted business and seemed to be on friendly terms with each other. In Moab, people often fought as they bargained with merchants, and shopkeepers had to stay alert or their goods would be stolen. Here in Bethlehem, there was an air of peace and friendliness in the market that she had never seen.

Finally she came upon a stall that had carts and many beasts near a covered shed that was fenced in around the animals. Even they seemed relaxed and calm as they nibbled on hay. She stopped near the vendor, respectfully waiting for him to finish his business dealings with another man.

Finally, he turned to her and with shrewd eyes, he looked Ruth up and down and then glanced at her cart. Ruth blushed and lowered her eyes shyly.

"My lord, I am here to sell our cart and ox."

The man walked around the cart and the beast, poking him and said, "This beast is starved, and he cannot pull a full cart. Your cart is old and has seen too much wear. You should pay me to take this off your hands."

Ruth had negotiated with Moabite vendors many times, but she felt very intimidated being in an unknown place. Even though the man was short and round, Ruth felt overwhelmed by his strong character and piercing eyes.

Choosing her words carefully, Ruth said, "Naomi, the widow of Elimelech, has just returned to Bethlehem from Moab, and she sent me to you. She said you would offer her a fair price for the ox and cart."

The man stopped moving around the animal and looked intently at Ruth, scanning her face as he considered what she had just said. He walked around the ox and came to stand directly in front of the girl with a frown on his face.

Looking up at Ruth he questioned her, "Naomi? You say she is a widow? This is terrible news! What about her sons, did they return with her?"

Ruth, fatigued from the stress of the day, felt a lump rise in her throat, and she couldn't speak for a moment as tears began to form in her eyes. Taking a deep breath, she finally said, "No, my lord, they too have died."

The man was shocked. He shook his head and clicked his tongue. With a softer tone in his voice he said, "I assume you were married to one of the boys, is this true?"

Ruth was afraid to answer his question for fear of what the man would do to her or Naomi. Deciding the truth would be known soon enough, she replied, "Yes, my lord, I am the widow of Mahlon."

"Do you have no family in Moab?" he asked inquisitively.

Ruth raised her head and looked at the man, softly saying, "My lord, I do have family but I could not leave my mother Naomi and allow her to return all alone with no one to help or protect her. She is now my family." Ike looked at Ruth for several seconds in silence while he processed what she just told him.

Ruth waited patiently for the man to consider all she had said. She wasn't sure, but she felt the man might have been momentarily overcome by emotions. At last, he spoke, clearing his throat first. "Do you have any more livestock?"

"Yes, a few sheep and two donkeys. Mother ...," she paused correcting herself. "Naomi asked me to buy fodder for our remaining livestock if you favor us by purchasing our ox and cart."

Ike raised his hand and called over a servant and instructed him to take the ox and cart and bring him a bag of meal.

He reached into a bag that he had looped over his body and pulled out coins, counting them carefully. Then he said to Ruth, "Tell Naomi the price I am giving you is the best I can do and still make a small profit for myself. As a gift, I am sending you home with a bag of fodder for your livestock."

Ruth bowed before him, thanking him profusely. Such kindness she had never experienced, especially from a merchant! The money was not much, but it was enough to buy provisions to feed them for a few days longer. Ruth knew she would need to find a field to glean as soon as possible, for what they had left would not last much longer.

Ike watched the young woman as she departed his stall, considering all that he had learned. He turned and called his servant over, telling him to watch the stall, and delay anyone who wanted to buy or sell any items until he returned. He needed to inform the city leaders of Naomi's return, and of the devastating losses she had endured—and warn them that she had brought a Moabitess with her.

Chapter 6

CONVICTION

> So Naomi returned from Moab accompanied by
> Ruth the Moabitess, her daughter-in-law, arriving
> in Bethlehem as the barley harvest was beginning.
> (Ruth 1:22)

The long-vacant house needed a lot of care, so it was easy to stay silent and focus on the work of cleaning and restoring Naomi's old home. The older woman was grateful her friends stayed away as she wasn't prepared to share the story of her life and losses in Moab.

Ruth followed her mother's lead and didn't chatter as she worked by Naomi's side. She knew that Naomi had a lot on her mind in spite of what seemed like a joyful reception from her people. Naomi's breakdown was heartbreaking for Ruth, especially because she knew that she herself was part of Naomi's shame. She could only hope her love and devotion would eventually be enough to soften her mother's heart again, regardless of whether or not she was ever accepted by the people of Bethlehem.

Ruth had never felt at home in Moab even though it was her place of birth and her family lived there. If she was forced to leave

Bethlehem for Naomi's best interest, Ruth didn't know where she would go, but she knew going back to Moab was not an option, only a death sentence. Ruth could only hope her mother would be able to help her find a position as a servant in a nearby city that might not judge her for being a Moabitess.

Several days passed, and one evening as the light in the sky faded, both women finally stopped cleaning and sat down in exhaustion. The house was mostly habitable again, and they both felt a sense of strong accomplishment.

After a time of rest, Ruth stood and, gently placing her hand on Naomi, she said, "Mother, please stay seated and rest yourself. We have fresh water and enough provisions for tonight and tomorrow. I know you are worried about our food, but please do not concern yourself. As we neared your home, I saw the barley harvest is in progress. Tomorrow I will visit a nearby farm and glean from as many fields as the landowners will allow. I believe your God will bless us with food and provisions."

Naomi tried to speak, but the words seemed to get caught in her throat, and her lips began to quiver. It had been an exhausting day, and Naomi's emotions began to overtake her. She took Ruth's hand and placed it on her own face and said, "Child ...," but her words became choked in her tears. Naomi knew in that moment this young woman was more than she ever deserved. She knew she had hurt Ruth when they arrived in Bethlehem, but not once did Ruth ever show anger toward her. She felt an immense blanket of shame envelop her.

Ruth, seeing her mother's distress, collapsed at her feet and grasped her hands. She cried, "Mother, Mother! What is it? What have I done or said to distress you?"

At this, Naomi began sobbing and kneeling down, she laid her head on Ruth's shoulder. Ruth had no words, but held her mother tightly and cried along with her as she whispered sweet words of comfort.

When she could finally speak, Naomi pushed away from Ruth and stroked her face. "My daughter, it is me who has brought distress and shame on you! Can you forgive me?"

The two women embraced again and allowed the pent-up emotions and fatigue from the journey and hard work to escape their exhausted bodies in their tears. Once the tears subsided, Naomi did something she hadn't done in a long time. She patted the floor next to her for Ruth to come alongside her. Holding her daughter's hand tightly in hers, she bowed her head, and Ruth followed along with her mother.

Naomi took a deep breath and exhaled those healing, heart-changing words, "Father God ...," Naomi whispered, and together they prayed, something they hadn't done in a very long time.

Chapter 7

BOAZ

Now Naomi had a relative on her husband's side, from the clan of Elimelech, a man of standing, whose name was Boaz.

And Ruth the Moabitess said to Naomi, "Let me go to the fields and pick up the leftover grain behind anyone in whose eyes I find favor."

Naomi said to her, "Go ahead, my daughter." So she went out and began to glean in the fields behind the harvesters. As it turned out, she found herself working in a field belonging to Boaz, from the clan of Elimelech.

(Ruth 2:1–3)

Naomi and Ruth lay side by side, facing each other on their mats, and talked long into the night about the barley harvest. Naomi told Ruth all about the planting and hard work, but most importantly she described the celebration and presentation of the first fruit of their barley at the temple. She explained how important it was to give a tenth of their best grain to the priests to care for them and honor God for his blessings. Their arrival in Bethlehem had been following the landowners' return from the temple. Now the real work to harvest the fields would begin.

Ruth realized the stories that Naomi told were bittersweet because in days gone by, it would have been her family presenting those first fruits to the priests at the temple and hiring harvesters to work their fields. All that had changed with the death of Elimelech and her sons. Now her mother would be relying on the kindness of her friends to allow them to simply glean from their fields and hopefully gather enough barley to feed themselves for the coming months or use to trade for other needs in the market.

Just as the sun was beginning to rise the next morning, Ruth quietly arose from her mat and began to dress. She looked down at her mother, who appeared to be sleeping soundly, and hoped she would sleep a bit longer.

These past days had been difficult for Naomi, and although she had offered to go out in the fields, Ruth had insisted it would only be her gleaning. Ruth did not want Naomi to face her friends in such a lowly position because she was certain it would put undue stress on her mother. Besides, there were still many things to do in their home, so Naomi would work on those tasks while Ruth worked the fields.

Ruth was tempted to kiss Naomi's cheek before leaving their home, but she didn't want to wake her mother. She turned to leave and Naomi spoke to her, "Ruth, stay with me today and go out tomorrow."

She smiled because she knew that her mother was afraid for her. She said, "Let me go to the fields and pick up the leftover grain behind anyone in whose eyes I find favor" (Ruth 2:2).

Naomi didn't speak for a few moments, then she sighed and said, "Go ahead, my daughter" (Ruth 2:2).

Naomi sat up, and Ruth kneeled down to give her mother a strong hug and kissed her cheek.

Ruth arose, picking up a small jug with water, but leaving the food that Naomi had set out for her. Then she stepped toward the door to leave. Her mother would need the food, and she could eat some of the grain that she gleaned from the field.

Naomi called to her, "Ruth, take food and water with you."

Ruth slowed long enough to respond, "I've got everything I need, Mother, even a scarf to carry home what I gather today." She stepped out of the home as the sun began to break on the horizon.

She had not traveled very far when she saw a group of men and women preparing to work. It was easy to pick out the man who was in charge, and Ruth stayed off to the side, watching him as he instructed the men and women on their daily duties.

After the workers moved toward the fields, with her heart beating rapidly, Ruth approached the foreman and bowed down before him. She said, "Good morning, my lord."

"Good morning!" He smiled broadly, responding with enthusiasm. Joris was middle-aged, strong and solid in stature, and had deep lines in his face from many years of working in the sun and the fields.

Ruth stood but kept her eyes lowered to the ground and spoke softly to the foreman, asking for his favor that she might glean from the field for this day. She promised to work hard but stay well behind his reapers and gather only from the sheaves, not disturbing his crew.

Looking at the young woman quizzically he said, "Who are you? I haven't seen you around this area."

Ruth answered honestly, carefully choosing her words as Naomi had instructed her. "I am Ruth, Naomi's daughter-in-law. We are just back to Bethlehem, and we are both widows. We have only a day's provisions left in our home, and we must glean from the fields for food." Even though Naomi had asked Ruth not to let the harvesters know they were almost without food, Ruth felt it was necessary to let him know the urgency of her need to work.

31

The foreman had heard from his wife, Mabbina, that Naomi was back in town and had brought a woman with her, but his wife knew nothing about her as she had been fully covered. But everyone knew that Naomi and her family had been in Moab these last ten years, so it was no secret this woman was a Moabitess.

Joris was very familiar with Naomi's family as he had been friends with Elimelech's foreman who now managed another man's field. His heart twisted at what Naomi must be feeling going from a rich landowner's wife to someone who had to rely on the kindness of others just for food to survive. He would have Mabbina make a cake and send food for Naomi and this girl.

Smiling at the young woman, he said, "Ruth, my name is Joris, and I am the foreman for the man who owns this field. You chose a beautiful day to work. As you can see, the Lord has blessed us with a good crop this season. Our master, Boaz, is not here in the fields with us this morning but as his foreman I see no wrong in your request, so let's get to work!" With that, he turned on his heels and headed to the field.

Ruth was stunned for a moment at his kindness and her good fortune, but she quickly regained her composure and followed behind him. She set herself at a distance behind the women who had already begun piling and wrapping the barley into bundles as the reapers cut down the stalks. She got to work on the edges of the field, mimicking the women in front of her as she gathered and bundled.

The hours slipped by as Ruth developed a rhythm of gathering and bundling the stalks, keeping her work close to the edge of the field. It didn't take long for her hands to become raw and her back to begin aching from the bending and stooping, but Ruth didn't mind as she was grateful for finding work quickly and near to her new home.

As the temperatures and the sun rose in midmorning, Ruth became thirsty, and her stomach rumbled for a bite of food. When she saw the other field-workers stop for a rest, Ruth did as well.

She would have loved to join the harvesters for a cool drink of water, but instead, she drank the tepid water she had brought with her. She found a spot in the shade and reclined and rested her aching back muscles that were unaccustomed to fieldwork.

After a few moments of gazing at the sky and watching the lazy clouds drift by, Ruth decided to roll to her side and watch the men and women whom she had been following all morning. It was a very cheerful group, and even though she could not hear what they said, she could hear the gaiety in their voices and the intermittent giggles from the women. Their joy brought a smile to Ruth's face and her features softened.

Although she longed to be a part of their group and to be laughing and talking with the other girls, her solitude did not overtake how very blessed she felt in this moment. She dreamed that someday she would be able to meet and be friends with other Hebrew women who could overlook that she was a Moabite.

After a time, the workers started moving about and took their places to get back to work. Ruth did the same, being very careful to keep her distance.

The afternoon got even warmer, but the warmth seemed to soothe Ruth's back as she pulled the stalks of barley and gathered them into bundles. The work was going along much more quickly than when she had started that morning. Ruth began to relax in the work and hear more than just her own breathing—specifically, she listened to the sounds of nature and the cadence of the women's chatter.

She knew they were all curious about her, and Ruth had seen more than just the women looking at her. In fact, she deeply blushed at the recollection of the looks the men had sent her way throughout the day. Ruth wondered how long it would be that she could work in this field before being forced for her own safety to move on to another field.

Suddenly, the conversations of the workers took on an excited tone. Ruth's ears perked up, and her eyes followed the direction of their looks where she saw a man approaching on horseback. From the workers' excitement, Ruth guessed this man was the landowner.

The man rode his horse directly to the foreman and very clearly she heard his booming voice greet them all joyfully saying, "The Lord be with you!"

All the workers bowed before him, and in unison they responded, "The Lord bless you!" Clearly the man was someone they all admired.

The man gracefully jumped from his horse and while holding the reins, began to assess the work in progress with the foreman. Without looking at the workers, the foreman waved his hands to the other servants, indicating they were to get back to work.

Ruth uncharacteristically stood still, holding stalks of grain in her hand and curiously studied the man. He was very tall and probably near the age of her father. He was extremely muscular, and it was obvious he was accustomed to being outside as his skin was tanned. Although he had on clothing that was similar to the other male field hands, his were of quality material. His hair was thick and dark, and he smiled as he talked with his foreman, which caused Ruth to smile.

At that point, the man's eyes landed on her. Her smile froze, and she felt an immediate wave of heat from embarrassment overcome her as she realized she was gawking at him! Her heart began beating so fast she was certain it was going to jump from her chest. She lowered her head and upper body in an immediate bow, and without looking at him again, she returned to work. Her breath was so choppy and rapid that she feared she would faint!

What was she thinking? A million fears traveled through her head as she knew he could have her removed from the field, and all her work could be lost for her brazenness! *Stupid girl!* she thought to herself.

Boaz was unlike many of the other landowners as he worked his land, and he had been known to help build homes in the area for loyal servants or young couples starting together in marriage. He was kind, and his servants were fiercely loyal to him because of his care and knowledge of their families. Not one of his servants ever had an illness or accident that Boaz did not see that they had medical care and provisions while they could not work.

Joris watched as his master looked at the young girl working the edges of his fields. Boaz passed his hand through his hair, and shading his eyes as he looked at Ruth he said to his foreman, "Who is that young woman?"

Joris replied, "She is the Moabitess who came back with Naomi from Moab." He told Boaz how she had approached him early that morning asking for his permission to glean from the fields. "My lord, she has been in the field and worked steadily from her arrival this morning till now, except for a short rest in the shade."

"Ah," Boaz replied. "I heard about Naomi's return with the Moabitess at the city gates a few days ago from Ike." Boaz studied the girl as she worked. Joris knew that Boaz was a man of honor and if words or comments had been made about Naomi's return that were less than flattering his master would never repeat them.

Boaz turned his head to look around at his own workers, and their curious glances at the young woman, especially from the men, did not escape him. He turned to his foreman and spoke clearly to him, "I am going to speak with her. In the meantime, I want you to tell all the men in our group that they are not to touch her, and they are to protect her as fiercely as they would their own sister.

"Let the women know that I will be instructing her to follow along with them for her own safety. I want her to eat and drink with our women so that she has food and cool water to drink. She will stay with your workers through the barley harvest and into and through the wheat harvest."

The foreman nodded his head and led his master's horse toward his workers to give them their master's instructions regarding Ruth.

***

Ruth was working frantically, and although she couldn't see who was approaching her from behind, she could clearly hear the sound of steps across the field coming near to her. Ruth took a deep breath and turned to face the man she knew to be the master of the field. She blushed deeply and bowed completely down to his feet, hoping her full humility would be in her favor even though she felt all was lost. Her only hope was to pray immediately to Naomi's God, "God, please be with me!" she cried in her heart.

"My lord." Ruth's words were almost inaudible as her face was completely on the ground before the master.

Boaz reached down and took her hand to pull her up from her prostrate position before him. Ruth's face flamed an even deeper red, and she kept her face and eyes downcast as she stood before him, the feel of his strong hand still evident in hers. Tears began to well in her eyes.

He could tell that the young woman was on the verge of crying, and so he quickly and gently said, "My daughter, listen to me. Don't go and glean in another field and don't go away from here. Stay here with my servant girls. Watch the field where the men are harvesting, and follow along after the girls" (Ruth 2:8–9).

Ruth's eyes flew open wide as she looked up at him, completely shocked at his words and the kindness in his voice and his eyes. He lightly placed his hand on the side of her arm and continued, "I have told the men not to touch you. And whenever you are thirsty, go and get a drink from the water jars the men have filled" (Ruth 2:9).

She was overwhelmed with his generosity and tears again pricked her eyes. At this, she bowed down again before him with her face to the ground. She exclaimed, "Why have I found such favor in your eyes that you notice me—a foreigner" (Ruth 2:10)?

Boaz replied, "I have been told all about what you have done for your mother-in-law since the death of your husband—how you left your father and mother and your homeland and came to live with a people you did not know before. May the Lord repay you for what you have done. May you be richly rewarded by the Lord, the God of Israel, under whose wings you have come to take refuge" (Ruth 2:11–12).

Barely able to contain her emotion, Ruth replied, "May I continue to find favor in your eyes, my lord. You have given me comfort and have spoken kindly to your servant—though I do not have the standing of one of your servant girls" (Ruth 2:13).

Boaz stood looking at her as she continued to bow before him, and he knew she would not get up until he left her. He said, "Tell your mother-in-law Naomi you will stay in the fields of Boaz through the harvest season and to take comfort that I will see to your safety." With that, he turned and walked back to his foreman who had returned from talking to the workers and was holding the reins of his master's horse.

Joris told Boaz that the workers had been instructed on Ruth's care; all would be as their master wished. Not one would go against his instructions, and Joris knew from this day forward that all the servants, including the men, would treat Ruth with respect and as family, teaching her and training her to work the field with them.

Boaz shook his foreman's hand, thanked him for the hard work completed thus far, and mounted his horse saying he would return at mealtime. Joris bowed his head in acknowledgment, and Boaz rode off.

***

The day passed until lunchtime approached, and the workers gathered together to drink cool water from the jars on the wagon.

Ruth, still feeling timid, stood back and drank the last of her water, which had grown warm.

Ruth was still in awe at what she had gathered just during the first part of the day. She couldn't wait to tell Naomi about their blessing and her encounter with the master of the field. Ruth knew she would have to thresh throughout the day and especially near to when the workers began to stop for the day in order to get her barley home. She was glad she had wrapped a large shawl around her waist this morning in anticipation of threshing.

Following the master's instructions, she had followed the servant girls more closely than earlier in the day, and now Ruth was close enough to hear their conversations. The women had giggled throughout the day about some of the men or had talked about their children. She loved the easy conversation among them and hoped to one day be able to become friends with some if not all of them and join their talk as she worked.

In the distance, Ruth heard the sound of wagons approaching. She looked across the field and saw Boaz approaching in a wagon that had several women in the back. Ruth was pretty certain that they were bringing food for the workers, so she started to leave and return to the side of the field.

One of the young servant girls came to her and said, "Please Ruth, our master has instructed us to ask you to eat with us. Do not leave us now as the food will be delicious and sustain you for the rest of the day." She shyly smiled at Ruth and said, "My name is Alitsa. I would be happy to have you sit with me."

Ruth was thankful for the friendly nature of the young Israeli girl, and she couldn't help but return her smile as she timidly followed her to the food wagon. Alitsa was almost a full head shorter than Ruth and quite round of figure. Her eyes were large, and her face seemed to be smiling all the time.

Everyone gathered around the wagon, and Boaz led the workers in a prayer of thanksgiving for the harvest. He asked a special blessing for the workers and finished by asking the Lord to bless their food. Everyone pressed toward the wagon, talking together and grabbing pieces of bread and bowls of liquid to dip their bread. Ruth again hung back from the group as she was still unsure of herself and didn't want to offend anyone.

Boaz approached her with chunks of bread and a bowl and said, "Please come over here and have some bread and dip it into the wine vinegar." Ruth blushed at being singled out among the group of men and women, but she did as the master asked her to do.

When she sat down, her new friend Alitsa quickly joined her. Boaz then offered Ruth and Alitsa some roasted grain. She was ravenous after the day of hard work, so she ate all she wanted but still had some left over, which she quietly tucked into her tunic pocket to give to Naomi that evening.

Boaz uncharacteristically helped serve many of his workers, but he also stopped to talk to most of the men and a few of the women. He asked after all of the workers family and seemed genuinely concerned and listened to their replies. It was easy to see why he was so well liked among the workers. Eventually he sat down and ate with his foreman, and although Ruth couldn't hear what they talked about, it was obvious to see the two men shared a strong and comfortable bond.

Ruth returned her focus on Alitsa, thanking her for allowing Ruth to sit with her. Alitsa was curious about Ruth, but she was certain asking too many questions before getting to know her would give Ruth the wrong impression. She truly wanted to be her friend and not just gain information for idle gossip. Instead, she began by telling Ruth about herself.

"I'm so glad you came to sit with me, Ruth. We are near the same age, and my mother always says the most important relationships a girl can have are with close girlfriends. She says once we get married and have children, it's sometimes the only thing that keeps us strong and patient!" Alitsa laughed a hearty laugh, and Ruth couldn't help but join her.

Ruth was still smiling as she softly said to Alitsa, "I would like very much to be your friend, Alitsa."

Merrily Alitsa responded, "Then it's settled! When other women ask, you must tell them your best friend is me! We will be together as much as possible during all of the harvesting. I can also have you come to my home to visit my family and see my twins."

At this, Alitsa smiled broadly waiting for the appropriate amazed response from the Moabitess. Ruth didn't disappoint Alitsa as she clapped her hands and said, "Twins? How wonderful!"

"Yes! Isn't it wonderful?" Alitsa said. "They are very young, only four years old, a boy and girl. The Lord certainly blessed me and my husband, Kemuel, with these children. I named our son Naam and his sister Naama, which means "pleasant" in our culture. They have been such good children from the very beginning. Now that they are weaned, my mother cares for them while Kemuel and I work in the fields."

Pointing over to the group of men who were standing together eating and talking, Alitsa said, "See the man standing over there with the curliest hair? That is my Kemuel." He caught her eye and nodded his head at her with a smile, and Alitsa returned the smile with a bold wave.

Ruth could not believe her good fortune in making a friend so soon. She would have so much to tell Naomi tonight!

Although his workers were still chatting and relaxing after eating their fill of food, Ruth quietly thanked Alitsa for her kindness, and catching the master's eyes to indicate her thankfulness for the meal, she bowed her head toward him as he stood with the men. She arose and went back to the field to thresh some of the barley she had gathered that morning.

Ruth moved slowly at first as her muscles seemed tight and a little sore from the morning's work and sitting for a period of time. She hoped the threshing would loosen her muscles quickly.

Boaz watched her depart to the edge of the field, gathering the piles of barley she had put together. Then she spread out the shawl that had been tied around her waist. Picking up a large stone, she began to thresh the barley she had gathered.

He nodded his head toward Ruth and gave these orders, "Even if she gathers among the sheaves, don't embarrass her. Rather, pull out some stalks for her from the bundles and leave them for her to pick up, and don't rebuke her" (Ruth 2:15–16). Boaz wanted Ruth to return home with quality barley, not just the sparse stalks from the edge of the field, and he also wanted her to have more than enough.

So Ruth gleaned in the field until evening. She noted that the men began to leave stalks of barley for her that were heavily laden with grain. Ruth knew that she and Naomi were being blessed by Boaz. She stopped gathering before the other field-workers stopped so she could thresh all that she had gathered that day. Ruth gathered the barley into a bundle and threw it over her back to carry home. Before leaving, she waved to the women and told her new friend Alitsa that she would be back again in the morning.

Alitsa smiled at Ruth and said, "I see the Lord has blessed you!"

Ruth said with earnest, "Your God and your master together have blessed me this day. Today I have more than enough. I have the kindness of your master and his workers, and I have a new friend. I am very blessed indeed!" Ruth felt her heart would nearly burst she was so overcome by the kindness.

Without warning Alitsa reached over and gave Ruth a big hug and said, "I will see you tomorrow, Ruth!"

Chapter 8

PAINFUL MEMORIES

O my anguish, my anguish! I writhe in pain. Oh,
the agony of my heart!

(Jeremiah 4:19)

Still half lying on her mat, Naomi watched Ruth as she left, and
she whispered softly, "God, please let her find a safe place to glean
today. I ask for your hand of protection to be on her."

She arose and stood at the open doorway and watched Ruth
until she disappeared over the horizon. Taking a deep breath, she
turned back inside and closed the door.

There was still much to do, including washing, which meant
leaving her home and going down to the river. Washing clothes
was a skill that Naomi had to learn to do after her husband
died. Before then, she had always had a servant to do it for her.
Naomi stood looking at the clothing that needed to be washed
and decided that maybe tomorrow would be a better day for that
task.

With a resolute heart she went to work, first caring for the
livestock, then picking up the broom, she went on the roof to
sweep and clean. They needed a threshing and grinding area set

up, and it would be best if that could be accomplished before the sun made the rooftop too warm. Naomi worked until lunchtime and stood back to look at her hard work. It was good. She grunted out loud with approval and went downstairs to wash the dirt and grime from her face and hands.

After washing, she decided to sit and rest with a nice cool drink of water before she ate a few bites of food. There was not much food left, so a few bites would be all she would allow herself. Naomi had encouraged Ruth to take food with her today, and she noticed the girl had left her portion behind for Naomi. Shaking her head, she would remind the girl that she would need to eat in order to have the strength to work the fields. Hopefully Ruth was able to glean enough barley for them to have food for a few days.

Sitting on her mat in the eating area that was almost bare of food and wine, she leaned her tired back up against the wall and looked around her old home. This home was the place where she had come when she married Elimelech. It seemed to the older woman that no time had passed before she had quickly given birth to two sons in this home.

Leaving this home and her people had been the hardest thing she had ever done, but her husband said they would be leaving for a better life in Moab because of the famine in Bethlehem. She pleaded with him to stay and pray and work with the people to change their sinful ways to regain God's favor, but Elimelech was not willing to admit his failures or to help change anything unless it was a direct benefit to him. It grieved Naomi to think such harsh thoughts about Elimelech, but she knew her thoughts were true even though she never spoke them aloud to anyone out of respect for her husband.

Many other memories began to flood her thoughts, and without warning tears began to stream down her cheeks as she remembered better days. Closing her eyes she could clearly see her sons running in and out of the house and almost hear their merry laughter. There had been servants to care for her home and their needs, which left her free to do light gardening, shop, visit with her friends, or play with her children. Now, she and Ruth were destitute widows, relying on the kindness of those whose hearts would be softened toward them.

Sobs wracked her body, and Naomi thought her heart would break from the pain of the memories and the hard life that she knew she and Ruth would have to endure from this point forward. Maybe coming home was a mistake, she thought to herself.

Crying out loud, she wailed her heartache and pain; pain that had been bottled up for too long. "God! God! This life you have dealt me is too hard. I don't think I can go on, God. You have taken everything from me—everything!" And she sobbed until she was exhausted. Taking deep breaths, Naomi closed her eyes and eventually she drifted off to sleep.

She awoke with a start to the sound of a wagon outside her home. Feeling too tired to get up to see who it was, she stayed seated leaning against the wall, hoping whomever it was would just leave and go away.

There was a gentle tapping on the door and a soft voice said, "Naomi?"

Naomi froze, recognizing the voice of her old friend Varda, and her embarrassment and exhaustion from the emotions were too great to get up to receive her. She could not see her, not in these horrible circumstances!

But Varda was never a timid woman, and she knew that Naomi would most likely not answer her knock, so she opened the door and looked into the inner room. For a minute because of the bright sunlight outside and the dimness of the inner room, she did not see Naomi, who remained still as she leaned against the wall. When her vision adjusted to the darkness of the room, she saw her friend Naomi, and her heart broke.

Varda stepped back outside and spoke softly to someone, then she came back into Naomi's home, closing the door behind her. "Naomi ...," her friend spoke her name again, this time with a gentle softness. She crossed the room and knelt in front of Naomi and took her friend into her arms. Naomi began to cry again, and Varda spoke comforting words to her and rubbed her hair and stroked her back. "Yes, yes, my friend, cry. It is good to cry."

Naomi didn't think after all her earlier sobs and wails that she had any tears left, but the love and comfort from her friend brought tears afresh.

Naomi and Varda had been the best of friends growing up, and they raised their children together. Leaving Varda when Elimelech decided to move to Moab was one of the hardest things Naomi had to give up. Varda was similar in size and coloring to Naomi, and although her hair was very straight, she had the same streaks of white through her hair as well. They were so often together and so much alike in looks that many strangers thought they were related. This very much pleased both women, and they had commonly referred to themselves as sisters.

Yet the friendship and bond between the two women had been marveled at by many as they were so different. Varda was very compassionate and her emotions ran high from laughter to tears at a moment's notice. Naomi had always been practical and sensible, and emotions did not come as easily for her. But Varda knew a softness and gentleness in Naomi that most didn't take time to learn about her. It was their differences that kept the women close and accountable, especially after they married and had children.

Finally Naomi's practicality took over, and she pushed herself away from Varda. Wiping her eyes, she said, "My goodness, what a terrible way to greet a dear friend, and after working on the roof, I must smell like my donkey."

Varda laughed out loud and said, "I wondered where my dear friend had gone, but with these sensible words, I see you now!" She gave Naomi another strong hug and said, "Beloved, I don't care if you smell like one of the livestock; my heart is happy to see you again!"

With those words, Varda stood and extended her hand to her friend to help her stand as well. "I have brought you gifts for your return! I know your journey must have been difficult, so I have some loaves of bread, wine and milk, and many other things that I think will make your homecoming sweet."

Naomi started to protest, but Varda held up a hand to her and asked, "You would deny me this joy? Surely you would not deny me doing what I know you would do for me, Naomi?" She cocked her head sideways and looked at Naomi with wide and questioning eyes.

Smiling, Naomi said, "No, I will not deny you this, Varda, and whatever you bring to us today, we will gladly and humbly accept because I know it is all given with love from my friend."

Varda could not contain herself any longer, and she squealed and said, "It is! Wait until you see what I brought!" She turned to the door and went outside, commanding her servants to begin bringing in the items.

Naomi could not believe her eyes! Her friend had gone all out for her return. There was lamb stew, which made her stomach rumble as she suddenly realized she had not eaten all day. The bread was fresh, and the smell of it filled her home. Her manservant brought in a pottery jar of wine and another with sweet milk.

Varda was so happy that she was nearly jumping for joy, and each time Naomi exclaimed her pleasure, Varda would clap her hands in excitement.

After the wagon was unloaded, Varda instructed her maidservant to take Naomi's laundry to the river and wash it for her. She had her manservant unload hay and feed for the livestock and put it in the stable. Then she had him start repairs on the exterior so that Naomi's home would begin to look more like the home she left and not the mess it looked right now. Naomi was speechless and didn't argue, but instead she just allowed Varda to take full control of everything.

Varda turned to Naomi and said, "There are so many things I missed after you left, Naomi. I wept for weeks and was nearly inconsolable. Today we make up for some of that lost time as we have lunch together. Truly sharing our hearts together as we ate was the thing I missed the most. I hope you have not already eaten?"

Naomi said nothing for a few seconds; instead she hugged her friend tightly. If Varda only knew that without this food today, she and Ruth might not have been able to eat tomorrow. Choking back tears, Naomi shook her head and said, "No, I have not eaten, and I can think of nothing better than renewing our friendship over lunch."

Varda ordered Naomi to sit down and said, "I know it is your home, but I insist on serving you today."

Naomi, fatigued from the morning work, her spent emotions, and lack of food, didn't argue with her friend. Varda served glasses of wine, tore off large chunks of bread, and then poured soup into bowls. Sitting down beside her friend, she said, "Let us give thanks to God for our food and for bringing my dear friend Naomi back to our homeland and into my heart." Holding hands and bowing their heads, Varda prayed the blessing.

"Now," Varda said, "don't hold back; tell me everything as we eat."

Naomi was ravenous and ate and talked about all that had happened in the last ten years. She poured out her heart like she had not done since they last saw each other. Varda listened well; she laughed over the antics of the boys in the new town, then cried over her friend's losses and marveled at the devotion from Naomi's daughter-in-law Ruth.

It was midafternoon when Varda finally stood to leave her friend. Taking her hands, she said, "I will return, and we will see each other regularly as we did before, Naomi. I know things are different with your husband and sons now gone, so please give me the pleasure of helping you." Varda looked into her friend's eyes, and Naomi knew that she spoke with true love and sincerity.

Naomi, again overcome with emotion, nodded her head silently, agreeing to her friend's desire to help them.

Varda gave her another strong hug and promised to return in a few days after Naomi had been able to get rest and become more settled into her home. "Anything that you need, my friend, I shall be offended if you do not come to me first and ask." With that, she climbed into the wagon with the assistance of her manservant, and she waved a cheery good-bye to her friend.

Naomi stood at the doorway and waved back, thanking her for everything, including the work provided by her servants. She had not realized until that moment how much work the house was going to take on the exterior until she saw how much better it looked.

Looking around at her home and the laundry waving in the breeze on the roof, Naomi felt something that she hadn't felt in a long time: *hope*. She had hope that everything was going to be better now that she was home. Naomi went into her home to put away the food and clean up from their meal, but before doing that, she dropped to her knees and gave thanks to the Lord.

Chapter 9

STRONG FOUNDATIONS

> He defends the cause of the fatherless and the
> widow, and loves the alien, giving him food and
> clothing.
>
> (Deuteronomy 10:18)

Boaz rocked gently in the saddle as he rode to his parents' home
for the evening. It had been a great day, and the harvest was going
well.

The biggest surprise of the day was seeing Ruth gleaning in
the field after he had heard about Naomi's return from Galon
and Ike at the city gate. Galon's wife, Varda, had seen Naomi
return alone with only the girl, and Ike told of meeting Ruth in
the market and the details of the women's losses. The men were
all amazed the girl had left her family to come to Bethlehem with
Naomi.

Galon said Varda would be visiting Naomi today to bring
provisions and to rekindle her friendship as well as to gain details
about what had happened. If anyone could get details from Naomi,
it would be Varda, as she was a kind and compassionate woman.

Boaz remembered the day that Elimelech had left with his family, and a frown crossed his face. The men had repeatedly tried to talk Elimelech out of leaving Bethlehem for Moab, but the man was steadfast in his decision. Boaz had always thought that Elimelech gave himself more credit than he ought, and his nature was pompous, lazy, and selfish. He had not been missed at the city gate meetings during the last ten years.

Still, as he considered Naomi, he was sorry for her losses, especially for her sons. He knew that his own mother would be inconsolable if something happened to him.

Boaz was also certain after telling the men in his employ they were to keep Ruth safe, it would be a matter of days before the entire city knew about his orders. He hoped his standing in the community would be enough to keep her safe. As a foreigner in Israel, she could and probably would be subjected to scorn and disgrace. Hadn't his own mother been a victim of that same abuse years ago before she married his father? It was the pain of those years that caused Boaz to be firm in his decision to protect the girl as much as he could. In fact, he was on his way to his mother and father's home tonight to tell them about Naomi and Ruth. He knew his mother would wish to extend a warm welcome to the women.

Boaz gave his horse to the servants and walked into the entryway of his parents' home. At this hour, he was certain his parents were in the garden, and their servant confirmed this. The man escorted Boaz to the garden, then bowed as he left.

His mother, Rahab, stood up with arms extended to greet him. "Boaz! What a lovely surprise!" She gave him a strong hug and Salmon, his father, also warmly embraced him. Rahab kept her arm around her son's waist and walked him to the garden bench where she and her husband had been seated. "Please join us, my dear." And she raised her hand to her maidservant to bring another glass of wine.

Rahab and Salmon were advanced in their years, but both were strong physically and looked younger than they were. Rahab still wore her long, white hair braided and over one shoulder, which gave her a youthful appearance. Her attire was simple and elegant, and she maintained the curves of her youth.

Salmon was an older version of Boaz, and there was no mistaking they were related in spite of the older man's thick, white hair. Both father and son had thundering voices, yet their words were low and gentle, and the older man still moved with agility in spite of his age.

Salmon said, "Are things well, Son? I didn't expect to see you for weeks since the harvest season just began. What brings you to us so soon?"

Boaz replied, "It's true, we have only been at it for a few days, but I had an interesting conversation recently with Galon and Ike that I wanted to share with you."

"Oh?" his father asked as he handed him the wine that was brought by the servant.

Rahab stood and put her hand on her son's shoulder and said, "Before you two become mired in business, Boaz, will you join us for dinner? If so, please excuse me while I let the cook know."

"Actually, dinner would be wonderful, Mother, but I'd like you to stay to hear the news that I have to share."

Rahab raised her brows in surprise, then signaled for her handmaid and asked her to let the cook know that Boaz would be joining them for dinner. She sat down next to Boaz again and patted his leg to resume talking.

"You should know Naomi is back in town." He looked at his father and saw surprise cross his face.

"Elimelech?" Salmon asked.

"Naomi came back without him or her sons; all have perished." Boaz stopped for a moment, then continued. "She did not come alone; she brought a young Moabitess with her. Her name is Ruth, and she is a daughter-in-law to Naomi. Ike spoke with the girl in the market when she came to him to sell their ox and cart, and she told him that she and Naomi were widows."

"Oh dear," Rahab said with sadness in her voice. Although she had never experienced loss like Naomi, she knew full well what it was like to be a foreigner among the Israelites. Hadn't she herself experienced hardship and loneliness after she joined them at Jericho? It wasn't until Salmon, a well-respected man among the Jews, announced his intentions to marry her that she was generally accepted into the community. Even so, for a time some still remembered that she was not only a foreigner, but a former prostitute. Many scorned her to their deathbeds.

For a moment, Rahab became lost in her thoughts, and both men remained silent as she absorbed this news. When she left Jericho, she had walked away from her past. With each step she vowed to turn from her past sins and to trust the Lord God of Israel with her life and her future, even though she had no idea what that future held.

As hard as it was to not go back to the only way of life she knew that brought her wealth and favor, she knew she could not go back because God had spared her life and the lives of her family. He rescued her from the destruction of Jericho and brought her out from the pit of hell when no one else had done that for her.

She was thankful for the forgiveness of the God of Israel and wondered at times why God's people didn't exhibit the same forgiveness over past mistakes, especially when that person had turned from his or her sins. But in the end, she knew the answer: they were nothing but mere men and women just like her, with so many failures themselves. She knew sometimes it was easier to focus on another's shortcomings than face your own.

As it was, over time many people had forgotten about her past, and God restored the broken years of her life by giving her a sense of peace and contentment that she had never known. She was blessed that Salmon had married her, and she loved him deeply.

Then God blessed her again by giving her this son, Boaz, when she thought she was too old to have children.

In her heart, she knew had she remained unmarried and without children, she would have been just as content because God had given her all she needed and yearned for from the inside out.

The years and Salmon's love and loyalty had been good to her. In the beginning, Rahab remembered the loneliness and the men who initially had tried to force her to return to her former occupation. Joshua, the Israeli leader at that time, put a stop to the harassment and commanded that she and her family be protected. Once she married Salmon, most of the persecution stopped, and she never forgot Joshua's kindness and favor.

Rahab's maidservant broke the silence by announcing dinner was prepared. Salmon walked over to his wife, the woman who had captured his heart so many years ago. He placed his arm around her waist and softly said, "Come, let us continue this conversation at dinner." As they reclined at the table, the family withheld their previous conversation until all had left the room save the servant who attended to them.

Salmon gave a short and heartfelt blessing over God's provision for their table and the bountiful harvest. Afterward, Boaz picked up the conversation again by telling them that when he went to the fields today to oversee the harvest, he had seen a stranger in the field, only to learn that it was Ruth, Naomi's daughter-in-law. He touched his mother's hand and said, "I have instructed my workers to protect her and to also pull out stalks from the bundles so that she doesn't only have barley from the sheaves. I told the men to be discreet and not embarrass her as they do this."

Rahab's face beamed with a smile. She had never felt such pride for her son as she did this moment. Squeezing his hand she said, "You are a good man and a treasured son, Boaz. I know this is done from the kindness of your heart but also in remembrance of me. Thank you."

Salmon felt a tightness in his throat for his son's kindness, and with pride he said, "God's blessing on you, Son, for extending mercy to this girl and to Naomi." With a deep clearing of his throat, an attempt to recover from his moment of emotion, the older man added, "What else can we do for them? Surely they have many needs coming back from such a long journey?"

Boaz smiled broadly at his parents whom he loved so much. If he had goodness in his heart and life, it was because they mirrored such behaviors to Boaz his entire life. "I am not sure, Father, but I suspect what you say is true. I will see Galon at the city gate in the morning and learn more after Varda's visit today with Naomi. Once I have his report, we can all specifically help where she needs it the most. Thank you for your generosity."

Rahab was deep in thought, and she said, "I believe I will plan a visit this week and bring both women special gifts to brighten their home and maybe a meal or two from our kitchen."

For the remainder of the evening, conversation flowed smoothly about the harvest and other family business issues. Salmon had recently stopped laboring alongside his son because of his age, but he was still very much involved.

The hour became late. Boaz finally stood from the table and bent and kissed his mother and then his father. "I must be leaving or I will be late arriving in the fields tomorrow. Thank you for the wonderful meal, and I will return in the next few days to give you an update."

Chapter 10

BLESSINGS

Her mother-in-law asked her, "Where did you glean today? Where did you work? Blessed be the man who took notice of you!"

Then Ruth told her mother-in-law about the one at whose place she had been working. "The name of the man I worked with today is Boaz," she said.

"The Lord bless him!" Naomi said to her daughter-in-law. "He has not stopped showing his kindness to the living and the dead." She added, "That man is our close relative; he is one of our kinsman-redeemers."

(Ruth 2:19–20)

Naomi was heating the stew that she had enjoyed earlier with Varda when she heard the girl come into the house. She turned to greet her and to hear about her day, and her eyes flew open wide when she saw the large amount of barley Ruth had bundled in her shawl.

"Ruth!" she exclaimed. "Where did you work today? There must be an ephah of barley in this cloth! Blessings upon the man who took notice of you!"

Then all at once her heart went cold with fear and her stomach felt sick. Naomi knew how local men treated foreigners, and she felt sick over what Ruth may have had to endure to bring home such a bounty. "You must tell me everything that happened today. Have you been harmed?"

Ruth placed the bundle of barley on the floor and crossed the room quickly to embrace Naomi. "No, Mother, I am not harmed! The name of the man I worked with today is Boaz. He was very kind to me and instructed me to stay with his workers through the barley and wheat harvest. He told me that he would see to my protection and that I am to stay close to his women workers. ... And, Mother." Ruth smiled shyly. "I made a friend today too."

She slowly walked her mother to the mat so that she could sit down. "Boaz?" Naomi whispered his name.

Then she grabbed Ruth's hands and said, "Boaz! The Lord bless him! God has not stopped showing his kindness to the living and the dead." She added, "You must know daughter that this man is our close relative; he is one of our kinsman-redeemers." Naomi was filled with hope for the second time that day, and she said to her daughter-in-law, "Do as he says and go with his girls, because in someone else's field you might be harmed."

Ruth's stomach made a loud rumbling sound, and both women laughed out loud. Ruth said to her mother, "I don't know what you have cooking on the fire, but it smells heavenly!"

Naomi regained herself and commanded Ruth to wash up as she rose to finish their meal. Ruth handed over her portion of the roasted grain she had saved her mother for lunch. Naomi looked at Ruth and said, "What is this?"

"I saved half of my lunch. Boaz also asked me to join his workers at lunch today. I knew we didn't have enough to eat, so I brought it back for you."

Naomi was astounded. Ruth had worked in the field from sunup until sundown, and Naomi knew she left with no food for herself that morning. Yet here she was offering half of her lunch. She bit her lips to keep from crying. Squeezing Ruth's arm she gave the girl a gentle push to the basin to wash up.

As Ruth was washing, she spoke to Naomi over her shoulder. "Mother, where did you get the provisions to make this stew?"

Naomi said, "It is another blessing from God. I have much to tell you about my day too. But first, we will give thanks to God for all that he has provided today." The women sat together on the mat, held hands and bowed their heads together.

Naomi spoke, "Father God, we thank you for the bounty that you have given us today. You went before Ruth and provided a safe place for her to glean today and through the wheat harvest. We thank you for this delicious food and for the gift of friendship that stands even through separation. Father, I ask that you bless this food we are about to eat to the nourishment of our bodies and bless those who prepared it for us. We also ask your blessing on Boaz for his kindness and protection. Amen."

Ruth's stomach made another loud grumbling noise and both women laughed merrily! Naomi allowed Ruth to eat while she told her about her day and the visit from Varda. She showed Ruth all that Varda had brought, including food to last for several days. She also showed her the clean clothing that Varda's servant had washed for her and told about the work done by her manservant on the outside of her home.

Ruth was as overjoyed as Naomi over all the gifts, but she was especially happy about the help the servants had provided for her mother. Ruth knew that Naomi could have done all of it, but it would have been a hardship on the older woman so soon after their long journey.

After her hearty meal and in spite of her best intentions, Ruth began to feel sleepy and her eyes began to droop. She had no idea she would be this bone weary after only one day of work in the fields. She made herself stretch her back and arms to wake up and rose to carry their bowls to the wash area.

Naomi saw the fatigue in Ruth's face and told the girl to leave the dishes for her to wash later. She suggested they sit outside together on the roof to enjoy the night air and sky before retiring for the evening.

The women took the stairs to the roof, and Naomi took in a deep breath and said, "I think I am glad to be home. The stars seem brighter to me here." And she chuckled lightly.

Ruth looked up at the sky, and she did think the sky seemed brighter and filled with more stars than she ever remembered seeing. In Moab, it had not been safe for women to be out after dark, so this was a rare treat for the young woman. Instead of keeping a nervous watch out for unsavory night activity, Ruth relaxed and listened to the sounds of the city as it settled in for the night.

They lived near town, and the once-busy streets were quiet. Ruth could see flickering lights from the oil lamps of nearby homes dimly lighting windows. Naomi watched Ruth as she looked around at the city and smiled at how beautiful she looked in the moonlight. She could see why her son had fallen in love with her as she had a rare beauty that began on the inside and flowed through to her outside.

Smiling, Naomi said softly, "I haven't seen Boaz in ten years." She leaned back against the warm roof stone and looked up at the sky. "He and several other men from the city endeavored to dissuade Elimelech from going to Moab when they heard of his plans."

Ruth didn't know what to say, so she just sat still and waited for Naomi to continue. Naomi looked away in the distance as she recalled those days. Days when life seemed so carefree until the famine came to their land. The prophets said it was a result of their disobedience to God, and she knew this to be true.

She wondered what her life would have looked like had they stayed. No amount of pleading or tears could dissuade Elimelech from his plan to leave. He had been a selfish and self-centered man, and as much as it pained her to think it, her sons had followed in his footsteps.

He had not gained the notoriety he so desperately wanted by going to Moab, nor the wealth. Naomi never stopped praying that he, and ultimately her sons, would see the destruction being in that foreign land was having on their family and return to their homeland. Unfortunately, pride and ultimately his death kept them from returning. By then her sons were grown, married, immersed in the Moab culture, and considered that terrible place their home.

Naomi looked back at Ruth with sadness in her eyes. "Tell me about Boaz, Ruth. Has he married?"

Ruth blushed and said, "I do not know, Mother. He was very kind to me today, and I am grateful."

"He was born kind," Naomi said. "I am certain he is married. He is younger than myself and was highly sought after when I left Bethlehem."

Ruth had no words and was grateful for the dark of the evening so that Naomi did not see her redness deepen as she thought about Boaz. Her late husband had been a very thin and weak man, and Boaz was just the opposite. The combination of his size and gentleness was something that Ruth was not accustomed to knowing.

Her father and brother were large, ruthless men, and she had suffered at their hands many times. She winced as she remembered the beatings she received, especially when either man had too much to drink. As a child, her mother had come to her defense more than once and had been severely beaten until she was unconscious for that act of kindness. Ruth always hoped they would be too tired to beat her afterward, but their anger seemed to have untold strength.

When Ruth became betrothed to Mahlon, the abuse stopped so she would not be bruised or scarred for her wedding night. Although the scars were barely visible on her body, Ruth had scars deep in her soul from which she wondered if she would ever recover. Thankfully, although Mahlon was weak in character, he was not an abusive man.

To shake these difficult memories Ruth said, "Mother, you called Boaz a 'kinsman-redeemer.' What does this mean?"

"It means that Boaz can help us from our impoverished situation by redeeming our land, Ruth. But, we will talk more about this later. For now, we will go to bed as sunrise will come soon enough."

Both women went back inside, and Ruth changed into her nightclothes as Naomi washed dishes. Then Ruth lay down on her mat where exhaustion overtook the girl, and she quickly fell into a deep sleep. Naomi changed into her nightclothes and stood for a long time looking at Ruth as she slept.

Softly she spoke a prayer aloud. "Lord, I pray that you open the doors for us as you work out your redemption plan through Boaz. I know there are no coincidences where you are involved, and it is not a coincidence that you took Ruth to this man's field today. I only ask that you protect her and keep her safe from harm and heartache. You know that she has suffered too much already. Thank you, Lord."

Naomi extinguished the lamp and lay down on the mat beside her daughter, where she too quickly drifted off to sleep.

Chapter 11

LIVING FORWARD

So Ruth stayed close to the servant girls of Boaz
to glean until the barley and wheat harvest were
finished. And she lived with her mother-in-law.

(Ruth 2:23)

The harvest season sped by quickly, and Ruth flourished. She learned to laugh with her new girlfriends and rejoiced with them over their husbands and children. She and Alitsa had become close friends, and Ruth was very fond of her twins, loving every chance she got to see them and cuddle with them. When she went to visit Alitsa, the children would run on chubby legs to greet her. She couldn't help but collapse on the ground to receive their hugs and kisses.

The men working in the fields who had frightened her in the beginning were now like brothers. Although they were quick to laugh at her as she worked to learn from them, there was kindness in their teasing. Ruth had confidence they would all lay down their lives for her if necessary.

The biggest change for Ruth was that she no longer thought of God as "Naomi's God"—unknown and unseen. Instead, she saw God as her God as well, active and working in both of their lives. Although he was not a God she could touch like the wooden statues of Moab, El Shaddai, the Lord God Almighty, was more real to Ruth than any of those statues had ever been in her life.

As she walked home from the fields, she couldn't help but compare her new life to her old life. When she was a young girl in Moab, her daily focus was to be as obedient as possible to her parents and at the same time be invisible. Being invisible meant that perhaps that day she would not be abused by her father or by her older brother as he grew in age and size.

When she was very small, she would try to hide behind her mother's skirts, and once she made the mistake of running from her father. His wrath was twice as harsh when he finally seized her. She also made the mistake of trying to be invisible when he punished her, but that just incited his wrath as he derived a twisted satisfaction from her cries for mercy.

Ruth's abusive childhood fostered a fear of men and made her timid about many things in her life. She stayed close to her mother, and she didn't make friends because she was filled with shame about her family. Everyone in town knew that her father and brother were deceitful and they drank and gambled too much.

When her father came home and told her that she was to be wed to a Hebrew, he spat after saying the words. Initially she thought he was trying to secure her future until she learned that the man she was to marry worked with her father and he had won her in a wager. Ruth was humiliated and brokenhearted.

Who was this man? Was he no different from her father? Was she about to step into a new home that offered nothing more than fear and abuse just like her family home? She had cried to her mother but knew it was pointless to ask for help with the situation. Her mother, after all, was the one who taught her to be invisible. She did nothing but encourage Ruth to dry her eyes and accept her father's decision.

As Ruth remembered the day of her wedding, she also remembered how terrified and weak she was from fear as she awaited the arrival of her groom. Her mother had spent months preparing her daughter for the upcoming wedding, discussing the importance of being an obedient wife and caring for her new home, hoping to calm her daughter. Yet the girl remained petrified from drunken stories her father told about Hebrews and their hatred for Moabites. He even hinted that she might be murdered in her sleep on her wedding night!

As the sun began to set in the evening sky, Ruth heard the voice of the man she was to marry as he and his wedding party shouted their arrival to her home, lighting the road with their torches. Her mother kissed her cheek and placed the wedding veil over her head. Together her family and friends, who had gathered throughout the day, began to follow the groom and his men back to the bridal chamber he had prepared for Ruth.

Once they arrived, Mahlon took her hand and walked her to the bridal chamber while the wedding festivities began outside the tent. Ruth remembered feeling herself begin to slip away, as a blackness started curling around the edges of her vision. Inside the tent, her husband lifted the veil and that was all Ruth remembered until she felt a cool, wet cloth dabbing gently on her face.

In the haze, Ruth could see a woman quietly ministering to her, but she did not know this woman. The woman spoke soft and comforting words to the frightened girl. "There, there, all will be well. It is just wedding day jitters; you will be fine. It is well, shhhhhhh," the woman spoke in an endearing and kind voice. A feeling of warmth began to creep into her hands as the woman began to briskly rub them with her own hands to return life to them.

When the woman saw that Ruth was awake and alert, she placed a hand on the young girl's face and spoke words Ruth would never forget: "Ruth, I am your mother, Naomi."

Ruth felt her fear begin to rise again as she looked first at the man she was to wed and then again at the woman. She clung tightly to the woman's hands and whispered, "Please ask him to kill me quickly that I may not suffer."

Naomi's eyes widened with shock, and she turned to look at her son saying, "This girl is half scared to death!" Looking back at Ruth, she said, "Daughter, I do not know what you have been told, but you will never be harmed in our home."

Just as Naomi promised, Ruth was never harmed by Mahlon. He was not a man of character, but he never abused Ruth, and she believed that he eventually came to love her.

Naomi took the young girl into her home and taught her how to cook and live according to Hebrew customs. Ruth did as Naomi directed, but she never fully embraced them as her own, only going through the motions to keep peace with her new family. When Orpah married Kilion, things were more difficult as Orpah was not willing to embrace the Hebrew customs. Orpah and Naomi often argued about the Moabite gods, and Ruth did her best to keep peace with the two women.

Now, the old days were gone and Ruth knew she would never see them again in her lifetime. Fear, once an emotion that governed her days and nights had lost its power to control her. Her ability to trust had materialized from the love and safety she felt from her mother and new friends. Each day she looked forward to work and to returning to her warm and welcoming home; all things she had never had or felt in Moab. Her new life was not easy, but it seemed easier knowing that it was God and not fear in control of her life now. She had never known how badly she needed love, joy, peace, and safety until she had them.

Ruth was amazed and grateful for the goodness in her life, and she thanked God daily for bringing her home, because surely Bethlehem was now her home. If nothing changed from this day forward until she died, Ruth knew she would have peace and joy simply because her heart now belonged to God, and she was living in a place that embodied all that was home to her.

There was just one small problem. Each day, in spite of God's favor, Ruth had a secret yearning in her heart that kept her from being content. Each day she told herself it would be the last day she would have these thoughts, and each day she awoke being overcome by the strength of that longing in her heart. She silently prayed daily for God to remove her yearnings and quiet her heart.

Chapter 12

NAOMI'S HOPE

Naomi was thriving as well and the two women had fallen into a daily pattern of work in their home. The older woman had long regained her confidence and ventured into her hometown using their abundance of barley and wheat to barter for food and supplies to store up for the upcoming fall and winter months. And even so, they had more than they needed.

Their home was cozy and comfortable and a reflection of the two women. It no longer reminded Naomi of days gone by, but rather it was a home filled with sweet memories of the past while she and Ruth created new memories and friendships beyond their dreams.

Shortly after Varda's visit, Boaz and his father Salmon came to see Naomi and supplied them with enough wood to last many months for their stove. Rahab, Boaz's mother, had also come with the men and brought new rugs for their floors, several bolts of exquisite fabrics for Naomi to make clothing for each of them, and many other personal and household items that Naomi had had to sell in order to make the trip back to Bethlehem. Naomi felt blessed that she was able to count Rahab as a new friend, a woman who was older and sensible and whom she could turn to for wise counsel.

She also discovered through her relationship with Rahab that her son Boaz was not married or betrothed to wed.

Yet with all these good things in their lives, Naomi knew that God's restoration was not complete. The time was drawing near for her to have a long talk with Ruth.

Chapter 13

RUTH'S DESIRE

Ruth walked slowly in the early evening dusk, deep in thought, laden with the last of her gathered wheat. It had been an extremely hot and hard workday as they all pushed to finish harvesting the last field. The harvesting season was finally over.

She knew that she should be happy that the hard fieldwork was finished, and she could help Naomi with separating the massive amounts of barley and wheat she had been bringing home daily. Yet instead of feeling happy, Ruth felt a deep sadness creep into her heart. It was true she would miss seeing all of her friends every day, but the sadness was about a secret longing that she could not speak aloud.

She only hoped no one knew or recognized her unrest. Even though Alitsa didn't say anything, she suspected her dear friend knew she was struggling with something internally. But Ruth would not share this information with her friend or anyone because it was foolishness. She had irrationally and hopelessly fallen in love with her master, Boaz.

Every morning, she looked for him to arrive in the fields and treasured every moment when he spoke to her or just looked at her or favored her with a smile. Boaz never showed anything but kindness to her, and she knew that she was wasting time allowing all those private thoughts about him before drifting off to sleep.

As she neared her home, Naomi suddenly appeared at the doorway, waving and calling out her name, with a relieved greeting. Ruth gave her a tired smile and returned the wave. Her mother continued to worry about her safety as she walked home alone, especially as the night was approaching.

Chapter 14

TAKING CHARGE

Naomi was pacing the floor of their home, looking for Ruth every few moments. Ruth was late arriving home today. She knew the harvesting was coming to a close for the season, and she knew that Ruth would be working late in the fields tonight, but she couldn't help worrying about her safety. Ruth was a beautiful, young woman, and it seemed to Naomi that Ruth appeared to have a special glow about her these days that made her look even more beautiful.

Naomi had seen this look before in many young women, even herself many years ago. Ruth was in love.

Wringing her hands as she nervously walked the floors of her home, Naomi wondered about the man whom Ruth had come to love. Knowing that Ruth spent time with the workers on and off the fields for months, Naomi was certain she had fallen in love with one of them. She wondered if at this very moment a young man was pledging his love for Ruth.

This would not do; it would not be an option for them, and as much as it broke her heart, she had to tell Ruth everything tonight. Naomi knew that Ruth's devotion to her was absolute, and she had every intention of taking advantage of that commitment. Naomi's heart quickened with guilt as she knew her plan would be risky and bold and might even bring Ruth and Naomi shame.

Yet Naomi felt there was no other way to protect their home and their future. In addition, she was tired of seeing Ruth toil and labor to exhaustion in the fields. As her mother, she felt it was her responsibility to plan their future and remove Ruth from working in the fields into a home where she would have security and care with no hard labor.

Naomi couldn't stand waiting for Ruth another moment, and she determined to walk down the road in hopes of meeting the girl on the way. As she was about to step out the door, she saw Ruth coming, the shawl on her back bundled heavily with wheat.

Naomi's legs suddenly felt weak with relief when she saw her, and she leaned back against the door frame momentarily for support. A deep breath escaped her lips as she waved and called out, "Ruth! Daughter, I am so thankful to see you!"

Ruth smiled back at the woman and raised her hand in greeting. Naomi met her daughter taking the bundle of wheat and hustling Ruth into their home, leading her directly to the bathing area. Ruth laughed and said, "Mother, what are you doing?"

"Quickly, get undressed so that we may bathe you and wash your hair. It is time."

"Time for what, Mother?" Ruth felt confusion overcome her as she watched her mother bustle about the room.

"It is time for us to secure our future, Ruth. Quickly, get undressed, I will talk to you as we bathe and prepare you for the evening."

Chapter 15

DARING PLAN

One day Naomi her mother-in-law said to her, "My daughter, should I not try to find a home for you, where you will be well provided for? Is not Boaz, with whose servant girls you have been, a kinsman of ours? Tonight he will be winnowing barley on the threshing floor. Wash and perfume yourself, and put on your best clothes. Then go down to the threshing floor, but don't let him know you are there until he has finished eating and drinking. When he lies down, note the place where he is lying. Then go and uncover his feet and lie down. He will tell you what to do."

(Ruth 3:1–4)

Ruth's heart was racing. She loved and trusted her mother, but this plan sounded risky and her pleadings not to go through with it seemed to have had no effect on Naomi's determination.

The evening was a whirlwind, learning about Hebrew customs regarding a kinsman-redeemer. She learned that according to their laws, Boaz had the right to redeem them and their property from their current state of poverty as he was a relative of Elimelech. It also meant that since Naomi was too old to marry, Boaz could marry Ruth, and if they had a son, he would carry on the family line. Ruth felt disheartened as she considered Boaz marrying her only as family duty.

It was not a woman's place to worry about any of this, but Ruth's heart longed for more than a marriage of convenience. She wanted a marriage like her friends Alitsa and Kemuel, who loved each other.

For a moment she wondered if she confessed her love for Boaz to Naomi if it would make a difference in her mother's plans. In the end, she decided that would only complicate things for her and Naomi. Her understanding about a kinsman-redeemer had nothing to do with love; it was purely based on culture laws. Whether or not she loved or liked Boaz was not relevant to this situation and their future care.

Naomi helped her bathe, and she fussed at Ruth as tears threatened to spill out of her dark eyes, commanding her to stop as she didn't want her to have swollen eyes. She lightly perfumed Ruth and rubbed her body with oil until it glistened. Carefully and gently, Naomi brushed, smoothed, and braided the girl's long black hair, entwining in silky pieces of ribbon as she braided.

Then Naomi helped her put on a beautiful new tunic of the softest greens that she had made for Ruth with her own hands. Naomi took a shimmery scarf and wound it around Ruth's waist, which accentuated her fine figure, then brought out a delicate pair of sandals for her feet.

Ruth knew the fabric, ribbons, and sandals had to have come from some of the things that Rahab or Varda had brought to Naomi. After months of being in mourning clothes and working the fields, Ruth felt conspicuous and uncomfortable in the finery.

Naomi stepped back and looked at her daughter with pride and love. Truly she was a beautiful woman, and surely Boaz would be able to see her with different eyes tonight! Taking a dark and large mourning shawl, she wrapped it around Ruth and told her to use that to keep herself covered in darkness and to stay close to the trees as she headed to the threshing floor.

Naomi explained clearly over and over again what the plan was once she arrived. "Go down to the threshing floor, but don't let him know you are there until he has finished eating and drinking. When he lies down, note the place where he is lying. Then go and uncover his feet and lie down. He will tell you what to do" (Ruth 3:3–4).

She explained how important it was that Ruth stay quietly out of sight until all the landowners had settled down and gone to sleep, lest they become confused about her presence there. She prepared Ruth for what she might see and hear if the local prostitutes came to see the men as they threshed the harvest. She instructed Ruth to cover her ears and close her eyes to anything that was unholy.

Ruth felt her cheeks redden, but she promised, "I will do whatever you say, Mother."

Ruth couldn't help but believe in these final moments before her departure that Naomi's consuming and growing love had made her forget that Ruth was a Moabite and lower than a servant! What if Boaz rejected her and treated her no differently than the local prostitutes? She shuddered at the thought and felt tears creep into her eyes again.

At last it was dark outside, and it was time for Ruth to leave. Naomi looked up into her daughter's eyes, and she saw nothing but terror. Her heart lurched, and she almost changed her mind, but she brushed the thoughts aside and placing both hands on Ruth's arms. Naomi closed her eyes and whispered, "Father, protect my daughter, Ruth, and bless us with your redemption. None have been more faithful to me than this child, so I ask for your favor tonight in every detail."

Chapter 16

THRESHING FLOOR

When Boaz had finished eating and drinking and was in good spirits, he went over to lie down at the far end of the grain pile. Ruth approached quietly, uncovered his feet and lay down. In the middle of the night something startled the man; he turned—and there was a woman lying at his feet!

(Ruth 3:7–8)

Ruth left their home and made the journey to the threshing floor under the cloak of darkness, and God was with her as she saw no one.

There was a lot of excitement in the central floor area where many women were cooking and the men were laughing and drinking, so she was able to slip in unnoticed. She had hidden herself in a remote area behind large bundles of wheat. There she could not be seen but was able to see everything clearly.

Finally the night became quiet as women left to return to their homes and the men began finding beds near their piles of grain. Soon the entire area was quiet except for the night sounds and the occasional snoring from the sleeping men. Ruth had not taken her eyes off of Boaz and knew exactly where he was lying.

She was thankful that none of the local prostitutes had come for the night, and thought perhaps it might have been because so many of the men's wives were there for the evening. She silently thanked God for this favor.

Ruth's knees ached from her long workday and from being crouched down for so long behind the wheat. Slowly she stood up and stretched her cramped limbs. Taking a deep breath, she prayed to the Lord God Almighty for his favor and then quietly made her way around the outskirts of the threshing floor until she was close enough to see Boaz. She stood in silence on the edge of darkness, barely breathing herself, and watched his chest rise and fall in rhythm until she knew for certain he was fast asleep.

Very quietly she stepped next to him, gently uncovered his feet, and lay down, waiting for him to realize she was there. Ruth was certain the sound of her pounding heart would wake him! She clutched her shawl tightly around herself in an effort to stop her body from trembling. Then she realized that the tightening of her body only made the tension worse. So she focused her attention on her body, starting with her toes and commanding them to relax. Ruth worked her way up her body to her neck and shoulders.

After some time had passed, Ruth—exhausted from the day of labor—felt herself begin to relax, and her eyes start to become very heavy. A long sigh escaped her lips as she began to drift toward sleep.

All at once something startled Boaz, and he realized there was someone at his feet. Sitting up, he whispered, "Who are you and what are you doing here?"

Ruth jerked awake and as she sat up in haste, her shawl fell away revealing who she was to her master. She knew there was only one way to answer his question and protect her reputation lest he be confused about her intentions. With confidence, she softly repeated the words as Naomi had taught her earlier that evening.

"I am your servant, Ruth," she said. "Spread the corner of your garment over me since you are a kinsman-redeemer" (Ruth 3:9).

Boaz looked at her in silence for a long moment, and Ruth could see emotions move across his face, but she couldn't read what was in his heart. She looked longingly in his eyes and wanted to reach out and touch his arm. Instead, she lowered her head and closed her eyes, waiting for her master to make his decision.

In a thick voice he softly replied, "The Lord bless you, my daughter. This kindness is greater than that which you showed earlier. You have not run after the younger men, whether rich or poor. And now, my daughter, don't be afraid. I will do for you all you ask. All my fellow townsmen know that you are a woman of noble character" (Ruth 3:10–11). He said this because he wanted her to know that even though this was a bold move, she was highly regarded by himself and others.

He continued, "Although it is true that I am near of kin, there is a kinsman-redeemer who is nearer than I. Stay here for the night, and in the morning if he wants to redeem, good; let him redeem. But if he is not willing, as surely as the Lord lives, I will do it. Lie here until morning" (Ruth 3:12–13).

Ruth's head snapped up and her eyes flew open wide in horror when she heard the words Boaz spoke regarding the other kinsman-redeemer. Boaz knew in that moment that she did not know about this man, and he watched as a series of emotions moved across her face. He kept his gaze on her, hoping it would give her comfort. At last she nodded her head and lay back down at Boaz's feet. He gently covered her, and saying no more, he lay back down.

Neither slept, and Ruth considered all he said to her. He had comforted her with the knowledge that she was well thought of and respected in spite of the bold move she made this night. He promised to see to her and Naomi's care whether or not it was through this other man or by Boaz himself.

Ruth cried out in her heart, "God! God! Please let my heart be at peace with whatever happens tomorrow, but God, I confess I love this man. I confess that the desire of my heart is to be with him, yet Father, I relinquish even this desire to you tonight. If this other kinsman redeems, I will honor you by my devotion to him; all I ask is that you remove this love for Boaz from my heart! God, please hear my prayer!" Tears quietly slid down Ruth's face.

Chapter 17

MAN OF HONOR

> Her husband's brother shall take her and marry
> her and fulfill the duty of a brother-in-law to her.
> The first born son she bears shall carry on the
> name of the dead brother so that his name will
> not be blotted out from Israel.
>
> (Deuteronomy 25:5–6)

Boaz lay still and listened to the breathing of the young woman at his feet. He was pretty certain there was a time when she was crying. He wanted to sit up and comfort her, but he knew that if he touched her, all his control would be lost. Ruth was a beautiful young girl, and in the moonlight she was even more beautiful, especially in her fine garments and with her beautifully braided hair. Her scent was about to drive him mad with desire. Not one piece of her beauty escaped him. He clenched his hands and forced himself to focus on what he must do as quickly as possible in the morning at the city gates.

He also knew he needed to get Ruth safely off the threshing floor before she was seen by any of the other men or before the city began to wake up. He focused on this plan and not the longing his body had to reach down and gather her up into his arms.

Finally the sun started peeking in the distance, and Boaz sat up and touched Ruth's arm gently. She sat up, and he placed a finger over his lips indicating they were to be silent. She nodded her head to let him know she understood his command.

He took her to a large pile of barley and softly said, "Bring me the shawl you are wearing and hold it out that I may give you some barley to take home to your mother-in-law." When she did so, he poured into it six measures of barley, and winding the shawl tightly so none would spill, he put it on her and whispered, "I don't want you to go back home empty-handed."

He walked her to the road and instructed her to stay covered in the dusk, following the side of the road and not the middle. "Go quickly, Ruth, so that you are not seen and before the city awakens." She quickly turned and started down the road as Boaz watched her until she melted into the morning darkness.

As he returned to the threshing floor, there was a man watching what had just happened. Boaz quietly approached him and said, "Be silent and don't let it be known that a woman came to the threshing floor."

The man nodded his head in agreement. He did not know who this woman was or what she was doing on the threshing floor as it was not a place for women of character. However, by Boaz's actions, he suspected she was perhaps someone in need because she had left with a large load of grain. He guessed she had approached Boaz discreetly before daylight in order to remain anonymous.

Boaz told the man that he had business to attend to in town, and he would be back soon to thresh his harvest later in the day. The men shook hands, and Boaz left immediately.

Chapter 18

TRUSTING GOD

When Ruth came to her mother-in-law, Naomi asked, "How did it go, my daughter?"

Then she told her everything Boaz had done for her and added, "He gave me these six measures of barley, saying, 'Don't go back to your mother-in-law empty-handed.'"

Then Naomi said, "Wait, my daughter, until you find out what happens. For the man will not rest until the matter is settled today."

(Ruth 3:16–18)

All night long, Naomi paced the floor of their home and prayed over and over for Ruth's protection. She kept asking herself if she had made a rash decision. Would Boaz have made the move to redeem them had she waited a little while longer? Would he now think of Ruth as nothing more than a Moabitess prostitute, especially because of the way Naomi had dressed and perfumed her? What if the other men saw Ruth first and misinterpreted her presence on the threshing floor? Would Boaz step forward to protect her, or would he allow her to suffer the consequences of this old woman's decision?

Naomi groaned and cried aloud to God, asking for forgiveness for her impatience. Her body became exhausted from the worry and pacing, so she sat down near the doorway of their home and leaned back against the wall to rest for a few moments. She continued to wring her hands as she prayed, but eventually fatigue overtook her and she drifted off into a fitful sleep.

Just as the light of day was beginning to peek through the windows, Ruth slipped into the doorway of their home. Naomi started awake and arose to greet Ruth. "How did it go, my daughter?"

Ruth handed over the shawl wound tightly with the barley to Naomi. "Before I left he gave me these six measures of barley, saying to me, 'Don't go back to your mother-in-law empty-handed.'"

Ruth walked away from Naomi and began to unbraid her hair and take out the ribbons and her long, black hair spilled over her shoulders. She began to unwind and fold the beautiful sash from her waist and slipped out of the sandals. Pulling the gorgeous tunic over her head, she lightly rubbed her hands across the fabric before she placed it across a chair and pulled on one of her old tunics. She sat down in the chair and began to brush and braid her hair.

Naomi approached her daughter and considered her silence as a sure sign that something was wrong. "What happened last night, Ruth? Please tell me."

Ruth slowly turned in her chair and her hands stopped twirling her hair for a moment as she looked at Naomi. The girl's fingers began to work in her hair again, and she didn't speak until her hair was fully braided. Placing her hands into her lap she said, "Boaz is not our kinsman-redeemer as there is another who is closer than he is to you."

Naomi gasped, "What? Who ...," but then she remembered and she closed her eyes as she considered this man. Ruth raised her hands to cover her face as she began to weep.

***

Naomi and Ruth sat facing each other knee to knee in silence. They had been sitting like this since Ruth had told Naomi all that had happened the night before and ended with the news that there was another kinsman closer to Naomi who had the first right of redemption.

Naomi knew this other man. Had she not known him while married to Elimelech? He was a good man, and very ambitious. Naomi also knew that he was married and had his own children. Because of the impact to his own heirs, would he choose not to take Ruth as his wife? Their future was much more precarious than Ruth even knew if this man chose to redeem only her property. For now, Naomi chose not to mention this information to Ruth.

Squaring her shoulders, Naomi took a deep breath and said, "We will not fabricate wild stories in our minds about this other man and what he will or will not do. Wait, my daughter, until you find out what happens. For Boaz will not rest until the matter is settled today."

Ruth could no longer contain her thoughts and she said, "But, Mother! What if the other man agrees to redeem us? Who is he, what is he like? Is he kind? Oh, Mother! I fear I will be in despair if I must marry this other man, for I must tell you that I am in love with Boaz!" Ruth knew she shocked Naomi with this news, but she wanted to tell her mother about her heartbreak.

Naomi didn't move for a moment, stunned by Ruth's confession. Exhaling slowly, she gathered the girl in her arms and patted her on the back, offering no words of comfort as both women knew they had no choice in this matter.

The two women embraced silently until Naomi placed her hands on Ruth's shoulders and pushed her away to look into her eyes. Naomi lifted her hand and placed the palm on Ruth's face and she said gently, "Daughter, in such a short time much has happened to us both," and she pointed her finger at herself and then back to Ruth. "Together we have learned a lot about the love of our God. Yes! We know clearly that God loves both of us!" Naomi spoke with conviction.

Naomi smiled as she continued, "We are under the protection of our Father's mighty wings, daughter! Look at what he has done for us in provisions alone!"

The older woman outstretched her hand and swept the rooms around them filled with piles and baskets of barley and wheat. Ruth allowed her eyes and body to turn and follow the direction of Naomi's hand. As Ruth's eyes took in the grains piled around their home, she nodded her head in acknowledgment of God's immense blessing.

Naomi put her hands into Ruth's and said, "We have much to be grateful for, Ruth. Let us not ever forget what God has done for us by shedding tears or doubting what God plans for us. It means we don't trust him, daughter, and we must trust that his care has been so perfect thus far that his care will continue in this situation as well. I believe this, my daughter. Will you believe it too?"

A small smile replaced the look of fear in Ruth's face, and she nodded her head in agreement. "Yes. Yes, Mother, I believe in this too. I am still afraid, but I believe in God's goodness for us. Perhaps we should give thanks now?"

Naomi's chest swelled with pride for her daughter. "This is absolutely what we will do!"

Hand in hand they walked to their prayer area to give thanks. They both knew there was power in speaking their Father's holy name and sharing their hearts with him.

Chapter 19

CLEVER PLAN

> Meanwhile Boaz went up to the town gate and
> sat there. When the kinsman-redeemer he had
> mentioned came along, Boaz said, "Come over
> here, my friend, and sit down." So he went over
> and sat down.
>
> (Ruth 4:1)

Boaz was the first at the city gate before any of the other men, and he sat waiting for them. All the way into town, he carefully considered the situation with Naomi and Ruth as he walked and prayed, asking God to prepare his words and his heart.

The situation with Naomi and Ruth had been on his mind for weeks, and not just because he knew he was a kinsman-redeemer, but because he had become very fond of Ruth, and he admired her quiet and good character. Still, it had been a shock to find the young girl at his feet, and he knew that Naomi had encouraged her to make this bold move. Rather than be offended, it signified Naomi's deepest trust in Boaz to do the right thing for the women.

However, there was the issue of the other man who had the first right to redeem the women. From the look of shock on

Ruth's face when he told her about him, he could only assume that Naomi had forgotten about him as well.

Carefully considering all he knew about this man, Boaz asked for God to guide his words so he didn't insult the man, but only spoke the truth. He wanted to encourage him to make the right choice should he choose to redeem Naomi and Ruth, which meant marrying the younger woman to produce an heir for the line of Elimelech.

He knew the man could choose to redeem the land but not marry Ruth, which would be a disaster for the women. He also knew in choosing to marry Ruth, this man's wife would be very angry. Boaz knew a woman could have a soft heart about someone's plight until it impacted her own heirs. A decision to marry Ruth would impact the man and his family, so Boaz prayed his relative would choose wisely should he choose to redeem.

Soon the men of the city began to arrive. They all greeted each other with comradery that comes only from knowing each other for many years. Galon and Salmon arrived together, and many of the men greeted Salmon with joy as he didn't often come to the city gates. In his older years, he preferred the company of his wife and the solitude of his gardens over politics.

Boaz was moved as he believed God had sent his father to him this day for support. When the time came for him to speak of Naomi's desire to redeem, he knew he would have Salmon's attention and support to encourage this man to do the right thing for the two women.

When the kinsman-redeemer arrived, Boaz said, "Come over here, my friend, and sit down with me." So he went and sat down by Boaz.

Boaz took ten of the elders of the town and said, "Sit here," and they did so. Then he said to the kinsman-redeemer, "Naomi, who has come back from Moab, is selling the piece of land that belonged to our brother Elimelech. I thought I should bring the matter to your attention and suggest that you buy it in the presence of these seated here and in the presence of the elders of my people. If you will redeem it, do so. But if you will not, tell me, so I will know. For no one has the right to do it except you, and I am next in line" (Ruth 4:2–4).

Salmon looked at his son, and although he spoke no words, there was a slight rise in his brows that only Boaz saw. Salmon had seen a change in his son over the past months, and he believed that he had come to love this young Moabite who was Naomi's daughter-in-law. In his heart, he asked for God to give his son the desires of his heart, just as God had given Salmon the desires of his heart with his wife Rahab.

The man said, "I will redeem it." Immediately the men of the city gate began nodding their approval and murmuring.

Holding his hand up for silence, Boaz then said, "On the day you buy the land from Naomi and from Ruth the Moabitess, you acquire the dead man's widow, in order to maintain the name of the dead with his property" (Ruth 4:5).

The man started to protest that he did not have to marry the Moabite woman, but suddenly felt the eyes of all the men of the city upon him, and there was silence in the group as they waited for him to make the right choice. Many times they all had spoken about Naomi and Ruth and all that the young woman had done for Naomi since they had arrived together in the city. Everyone knew the Moabitess was a woman of character and that she had even forsaken her own family and customs for their ways.

As he considered the impact marrying the young girl would have on his family and his wife's reaction, he said, "Then I cannot redeem it, because I might endanger my own estate. You redeem it yourself; I cannot do it" (Ruth 4:6).

Taking his sandal off of his foot, the man passed it to Boaz and said, "In accordance with our laws to legalize this transaction to transfer my right to redeem to you, I give you my sandal in the presence of the elders. Buy the land yourself."

Boaz took the man's sandal and standing before the elders, he loudly announced to them and all the people who were near, "Today you are witnesses that I have bought from Naomi all the property of Elimelech, Kilion, and Mahlon. I have also acquired Ruth the Moabitess, Mahlon's widow, as my wife, in order to maintain the name of the dead with his property, so that his name will not disappear from among his family or from the town records. Today, you are witnesses" (Ruth 4:9–10)!

Then the elders and all those at the gate said, "We are witnesses. May the Lord make the woman who is coming into your home like Rachel and Leah, who together built up the house of Israel. May you have standing in Ephrathah and be famous in Bethlehem. Through the offspring the Lord gives you by this young woman, may your family be like that of Perez, whom Tamar bore to Judah" (Ruth 4:11–12).

Salmon stood back, beaming with pride for his son. The elders all clapped his son on the back and continued to wish him well. Salmon nodded his head once so Boaz would know of his approval, and Boaz's smile grew. God had provided and he was good.

Chapter 20

A REDEEMER

A record of the genealogy of Jesus Christ the son
of David, the son of Abraham: Abraham was the
father of Isaac, Isaac the father of Jacob, Jacob
the father of Judah and his brothers, Judah the
father of Perez and Zerah, whose mother was
Tamar, Perez the father of Hezron, Hezron the
father of Ram, Ram the father of Amminadab,
Amminadab the father of Nahshon, Nahshon
the father of Salmon, Salmon the father of Boaz,
whose mother was Rahab, Boaz the father of
Obed, whose mother was Ruth.

(Matthew 1:1–5)

Naomi and Ruth spent the better part of the day sorting through
their barley and wheat, deciding how much they needed to keep
for themselves and how much they would take to market to trade
for oil, produce, and spices. They delighted in how much they had
and even believed they might be able to get additional livestock.
Both women were very excited as they discussed their future
market day.

Suddenly they heard sounds of an approaching wagon. Naomi and Ruth looked at each other, and they knew the moment was here. It was most certainly Boaz bringing them the news about their kinsman-redeemer.

Naomi said to Ruth, "It is God's will, and we will accept whatever he wishes." Ruth nodded in agreement, but her stomach was in sudden turmoil; it told the truth about the state of her emotions. Hand in hand they headed to the door together. Naomi stepped out first into the bright sunlight, and Ruth followed closely behind her.

Pulling up outside their home were wagons laden with supplies and all of the men and women Ruth had spent countless hours with during the harvest. With Boaz were Salmon and Rahab, who were in another wagon. Boaz went to that wagon and helped them down. He gathered his servants together, speaking words Naomi and Ruth couldn't hear, but they stood behind him and became silent.

Boaz and his parents approached Ruth and Naomi as the women bowed and respectfully greeted Boaz and his parents.

Looking from woman to woman, he boldly spoke these words: "Naomi, today I went to the city gate to speak with your nearest kinsman-redeemer. In addition, I gathered together the elders from the city as witnesses to our discussion and transaction. I told them that your property belonging to our brother Elimelech was for sell and explained that this man had the right as your nearest relative to redeem. As promised," he paused and looked at Ruth, "I told the man and the elders that if he did not redeem, I would."

Neither woman said a word, but Ruth stood straight and waited for the decision. She reminded herself that she would honor her promise to God no matter the outcome.

Boaz looked back at Naomi and gently spoke, "I am here to tell you that according to the law of Moses and of Israel, I am the kinsman-redeemer for your property. My servants are here today to begin the restoration of my redeemed property. In addition, I am leaving two of my servants with you today, Naomi. Obadiah will protect you, and care for your home and your livestock. Rhoda will tend to the inside of your home, cook for you, and be your maidservant. Whatever you desire, you need only ask of me as I vow I will care for you for the rest of your life."

Then turning to Ruth, he reached out and took her hand and spoke directly to her with tenderness, "Also, according to our laws, in order to maintain the name of the dead with this property, Ruth, daughter of Naomi, you are my wife!"

Without taking his eyes off of Ruth, he said to his servants who were murmuring excitedly behind him, "Please properly greet your new mistress." With this, the servants all respectfully and gladly bowed to her. There was not one in the group of men and women who didn't have the highest of regards for Ruth.

Ruth felt her legs begin to tremble violently, and she almost fell, but Boaz grabbed her arms and held her firmly. Looking into her eyes and squeezing her arms he said, "I will leave you now to allow Naomi and my mother to discuss and plan our wedding. Whatever you need, it is yours. I will inform the merchants in town you will be shopping. All I ask is that we not delay and that we wed as soon as possible. After all, I am not getting any younger!" With this, he broke into laughter and everyone joined him.

Ruth began to cry, but this time it was with tears of joy. God had indeed heard and answered her deepest prayers!

So Boaz took Ruth and she became his wife. Then he went to her, and the LORD enabled her to conceive, and she gave birth to a son. The women said to Naomi: "Praise be to the LORD, who this day has not left you without a kinsman-redeemer. May he become famous throughout Israel! He will renew your life and sustain you in your old age. For your daughter-in-law, who loves you and who is better to you than seven sons, has given him birth."

Then Naomi took the child, laid him in her lap and cared for him. The women living there said, "Naomi has a son." And they named him Obed. He was the father of Jesse, the father of David.

(Ruth 4:13–17)

Chapter 21

GOING HOME

This, then, is the family line of Perez: Perez was
the father of Hezron, Hezron the father of Ram,
Ram the father of Amminadab, Amminadab
the father of Nahshon, Nahshon the father of
Salmon, Salmon the father of Boaz, Boaz the
father of Obed, Obed the father of Jesse, and Jesse
the father of David.

(Ruth 4:18–22)

It was a beautiful day as Ruth sat outside under a tree that she
might be shaded as she watched her great-grandchildren play in
the field. She knew that her days were numbered, and she looked
forward to the time that she could join her love, Boaz, in heaven.
Until that happened, she wanted to enjoy every moment she had
left in the world.

Her youngest great-grandson, David, was toddling around
now, and he always seemed to be singing even though no one
could quite understand what he was saying. Ruth knew it was not
right to have favorites, but David was a true delight to her heart.
Holding out her arms, she called to him, and his wobbly legs

brought him to her. He struggled to climb into her lap until her servant helped lift him in the chair, and he snuggled up to Ruth. He laid his head on her chest and continued with his sing-song cooing.

Ruth wrapped her arms around the child and hummed along with him. She looked over at the child's father and said, "This one is going to be someone special, Jesse."

Jesse laughed and said, "Grandmother, you say that about all of our children."

"Maybe so ...," Ruth whispered softly as she kissed the top of David's head. But God had revealed to her in a dream that this one would someday be a king. She smiled to herself with the knowledge that God would reveal the same to Jesse in his own timing.

Ruth closed her eyes, enjoying the warmth of the day and the closeness of little David. Too soon, the child wanted down to play with his siblings. Ruth's servant helped him down, and she leaned back in her chair to rest. She felt her eyes become heavy, and she closed them to welcome the sleep that seemed to consume so much of her days now.

She recalled her life filled with so many moments of joy and laughter and yes, even sadness as those she loved passed away. She turned her face to look at Jessie and smiled lovingly at her grandson as she felt the life begin to leave her body. He returned her smile and touched her shoulder in loving affection.

Ruth closed her eyes again and she heard something that she hadn't heard in a long time. It was the sounds of a gentle whisper, wrapping itself around her body, softly calling her home. Ruth smiled and gave her last breath as the Spirit took her home.

87611413R00067

Made in the USA
Lexington, KY
27 April 2018